Samuel French Acting Edition

I0591878

Red in the Morning

by Glyn Jones

SAMUELFRENCH.COM   SAMUELFRENCH.CO.UK

FOR PRODUCTION ENQUIRIES

UNITED STATES AND CANADA
Info@SamuelFrench.com
1-866-598-8449

UNITED KINGDOM AND EUROPE
Plays@SamuelFrench.co.uk
020-7255-4302

Each title is subject to availability from Samuel French, depending upon country of performance. Please be aware that *RED IN THE MORNING* may not be licensed by Samuel French in your territory. Professional and amateur producers should contact the nearest Samuel French office or licensing partner to verify availability.

MUSIC USE NOTE

Licensees are solely responsible for obtaining formal written permission from copyright owners to use copyrighted music in the performance of this play and are strongly cautioned to do so. If no such permission is obtained by the licensee, then the licensee must use only original music that the licensee owns and controls. Licensees are solely responsible and liable for all music clearances and shall indemnify the copyright owners of the play(s) and their licensing agent, Samuel French, against any costs, expenses, losses and liabilities arising from the use of music by licensees. Please contact the appropriate music licensing authority in your territory for the rights to any incidental music.

IMPORTANT BILLING AND CREDIT REQUIREMENTS

If you have obtained performance rights to this title, please refer to your licensing agreement for important billing and credit requirements.

RED IN THE MORNING was first presented by James Madison University Theatre, November 15, 1988. It was directed by Allen W. Lyndrup, scenic design was by R. H. Roggenkamp, Jr., costume design was by Pat Kealey, lighting design was by Angela C. Warden, makeup design was by Gary A. Hicks, combat choreography was by Christopher Ockler, Technical Director was Phillip S. Grayson, Assistant Director was Cassie M. Chambers, Assistant Scenic Designer was Dawn Robyn Petrlik. The cast, in order of appearance, was as follows:

HELENA . . . . Shanon Wilson

JOHN . . . . John Chidester Harrell

BILL . . . . Brian G. Kurlander

EVIE . . . . Mary Szmagaj

DELL . . . . Ron Copeland

PENNY . . . . Jennifer Demayo

ROLAND . . . . Nicholas H. Rose

CAST

HELENA
JOHN
BILL
EVIE
DELL
PETERS *(voice over)*
ROLAND
PENNY

PLACE

A Victorian country house

TIME

1985 or thereabouts

RED IN THE MORNING

ACT I

SCENE: The conservatory and part of the hall of a rambling old Victorian Gothic house, a memorial to the railway baron who built it and in whose family it still remains. The conservatory is large and, as it runs along two sides of the house, L-shaped, the end of one part of the L being out of sight. The glass roof is supported by heavy iron beams, almost like a railway station in miniature, and its once white paint and masses of greenery are a distinct contrast to the dark wood and the gloom of the house beyond. But the conservatory is not just a place of plants. It has cupboards, including one which is very tall and a small wall cupboard for which EVIE has the key and which only she uses. The room has garden furniture, tables and chairs, mainly of the old fashioned iron variety. There is also a comfy shabby old easy chair and two-seater sofa. The place is heated by a wood burning or solid fuel stove. A door leads to the garden and, presumably, there is another from the hidden end of the L, and a pair of wide double doors lead into the hall where part of the staircase can be seen, and from where other doors lead into the rest of the house.

AT RISE: It is an autumn morning and there is no sign of life although, from somewhere in the house, a RADIO can be heard, one of the bright and breezy early morning disc jockey shows.

HELENA Enters from the garden. She is a woman of indeterminate age, probably late twenties/early thirties: a plain, bony face, no make-up; and an angular, bony body. She carries a trug and a basket of cut flowers. Putting these down on a bench top, she kneels to select a vase from the cupboard beneath it, remembers something, goes back to the door and calls to someone in the gardens.

HELENA. Oh Mr. Peters!... *(louder)* ...Mr. Peters!...I had to remind you... Well come a bit closer, man... *(She waits a moment.)* ...Madam said to remind you not to forget the hydrangea cuttings... Yes, hy... And will you be sure and do the irises today please? ... irises! *(Peters has got the message. HELENA nods and turns back to the bench and her flowers, taking a curved pruning knife from the trug with which to cut them.)*

(JOHN appears at the double doors. He is in shirtsleeves and wears a striped butcher's apron. He is a balding middle-aged man, about 40, fat and with a tendency to wheeze but, when he wants to, as light on his feet as a cat. At the moment he is just that, gliding silently up behind HELENA absorbed in her flowers. He stands just behind her for a moment and then:)

JOHN. *(quietly)* Good mor.... *(HELENA's reaction is swift and startling. She gasps, swings around and, in one continuous movement, slashes JOHN across the cheek with the pruning knife. At the same time the vase goes crashing to the floor. JOHN's hand flies to his face as he staggers back, doubling up to hunch into his wounded face. He takes his hand away to look at it. Both his hand and his cheek are covered in blood. HELENA has dropped the knife and stood stock still but now, as she sees the blood, her hands fly to her own face and she is almost incoherent.)*

HELENA. Oh, my God! I'm sorry ... I'm sorry ... It was an accident ... an accident! *(moving forward)* Is it bad? ... Here, let me look. *(But his hand goes to his face.)* Please ... please ... *(She tries to take his hand away but he moves back.)*

JOHN. Leave it alone!

HELENA. Is it very bad? Is it? Let me see. Please! *(He allows her to remove his fingers from his face, keeping his hand close to his cheek.)* I think it ... Oh, my God, it's deep ... It's very deep ... it looks ... it'll have to ... it needs seeing to. I'll call Doctor Selwyn.

JOHN. No. It's all right. It's all right I tell you. *(He turns as though to go back into the house.)*

HELENA. But you can't just leave it. Let me call Doctor Selwyn.

JOHN. No.

HELENA. But it might need stitches.

JOHN. I said no.

HELENA. What about tetanus? You should have an anti-tet...

JOHN. What the hell did you do that for?

HELENA. What? It was your own fault. *(JOHN stares at her, almost open-mouthed.)* Yes it was. You frightened me. I didn't know there was anybody there. It's my natural reaction sometimes, if anybody gives me a fright like that, my natural reaction to hit out. *(She takes a handkerchief from her cardigan pocket and hands it to him. He holds it against his cheek.)* And the ... it was ... *(She looks around for the knife, sees it and picks it up.)* ... it was in my hand. I was doing ... I couldn't find my secateurs. Peters says he hasn't seen them and ... *(JOHN sinks into a chair, holding the handkerchief to his cheek, his elbow resting on the table.)*

JOHN. You're a menace. You know that? Nobody's safe with you around.

HELENA. *(Drops the knife on the bench and gets a rag out of the cupboard to wipe the blood from her hands. She turns back to look at JOHN sitting in the chair.)* You're not just going to sit there. For heaven's sake, man, if you won't ... well go and wash it, put on some antiseptic ... band-aids ... *(She moves in to him slightly.)* ... I really am sorry. It was an accident.

JOHN. Was it?

HELENA. If only you hadn't crept up on me like that. I didn't hear you, you see, and ... Look, please let me call Doctor Selwyn.

JOHN. Jesus, woman! Don't go on. He's got better things to do with his time than drive all the way out here to look at a little cut.

HELENA. Little! *You* haven't looked at it.

JOHN. I'll do as you say, band-aid and all. It probably looks a lot worse than it really is. Satisfied?

HELENA. Of course I'm not satisfied. These things ... *the knife)* ... are hardly clean, are they? Garden manure, compost, insecticide.

(She breaks off as there is the sound of a MOTOR CAR outside. She turns to look towards the garden door.)

HELENA. Oh, no! That can't be them already. *(She glances*

at her watch and heads for the door to look outside.) They said they were making an early start but I didn't expect them so soon. Look at me, the state I'm in.

JOHN. I wouldn't worry. They won't even notice. *(rising)* Is it them?

HELENA. No, it's a van, a yellow van. The driver's having a word with Peters. Now what could he want?

(She turns back to look at JOHN but he has slipped away into the house. She sits at the bench, obviously still distressed at what has just happened. She still has the rag in her hand and wipes a spot of blood off the bench top. Inside the house the RADIO is switched off. HELENA gets up and kneels to wipe some blood from the floor and pick up the pieces of vase. BILL appears at the garden door: a big man, rough, cheerful, and about forty/forty five. He looks down at HELENA.)

BILL. Morning. *(HELENA looks up quickly, gets to her feet.)*

HELENA. Yes?

BILL. Telephone engineers. *(pause)* You called us?

HELENA. No.

BILL. Well somebody called us, reported your phone out of order. So where is it? The phone, missus. You want us to do it or don't you?

HELENA. *(pointing to the double doors)* It's just through there. But there's nothing wrong with it.

BILL. *(crossing to the door)* Is that right? Well, if there's nothing wrong with it, then we wouldn't be here, would we?

HELENA. I don't know so much about that.

BILL. *(Stops and turns to her.)* You what?

HELENA. If there *were* something wrong with it I'm quite sure you *wouldn't* be here.

BILL. Oh, I see, like that is it? Our reputation goes before. Well you got it all wrong, missus. We got a very good reputation, for speed and reliability. Must be the Gas Board you're thinking of. Had an accident have you? *(HELENA stares at him for a moment and then turns back to picking up the remains of her vase. BILL shrugs.)* Okay. *(silence)* The telephone, missus.

HELENA. *(fiercely)* I told you, through there.

BILL. Pardon me. I only asked. Are you a woman's libber or are you always like this?

HELENA. That is impertinent.

BILL. So. We live in the age of the common man, ducks. And don't say they don't come any more common than me because I already know it. I mean, something must've happened...

HELENA. What?

BILL. On a beautiful day like this you should be bouncing about.

HELENA. I do not bounce.

BILL. Well ricochet then. You should be full of the joys of spring.

HELENA. It's autumn.

BILL. *(He moves to the windows to take a look at the day.)* So what's wrong with autumn? A beautiful time of the year, if I may say so, and a most beautiful day for a beautiful time of the year.

HELENA. Are you here to repair the telephone or to rhapsodize on the seasons?

BILL. And do you want to know something? It's going to get better.

HELENA. What is?

BILL. The day of course.

HELENA. Is it?

BILL. You mark my words, better and better. On a day like this ... what can go wrong?

HELENA. Ha!

BILL. *(tapping his nose)* I know.

HELENA. You're tempting fate.

BILL. Superstitious as well are you? That is, apart from not liking my face. *(He has crossed back to the double doors, looked around the hall and found the telephone just inside the door. He lifts the receiver, holds it to his ear, looks at HELENA.)* Nothing wrong with it? Dead as a bloody doornail.

HELENA. Really.

BILL. *(Holds out the receiver towards her.)* Have a listen.

HELENA. It was working perfectly well last night.

BILL. Oh, I don't doubt you. But last night was last night wasn't it? And it's not working now, that's a fact. Right? So, if you 'ave no objections, I'll just get on with it. Okay? *(He puts down the receiver.)* Any extensions?

HELENA. Yes. Three ... four! ... three? *(counting them off on her fingers)* ... Kitchen, bedroom, drawing room ... study ... four.

BILL. What, no switchboard? *(His little joke falling flat he crosses back to the garden door.)*

HELENA. Now where are you going?

BILL. Look, are you sure you're all right, missus?

HELENA. Quite all right thank you. Why? *(BILL shrugs and turns away.)* How long will it take? The repair.

BILL. How do I know? It'll take as long as it has to, won't it?

HELENA. We're ... that is ... madam, is expecting visitors.

BILL. That's all right, they won't bother us. *(He is at the garden door. He puts two fingers in his mouth and gives a piercing whistle.)*

(EVIE appears in the doorway to the house.)

EVIE. What are you trying to do, young man? Shatter every pane of glass in the place?

BILL. Oh. Good morning, madam. Telephone engineers.

EVIE. I see. And you're trying to contact your friends at headquarters, are you? *(EVIE is a homely woman of about seventy, could be even older. In her youth she must have been extremely handsome in a hard way but the years have softened her and she now exudes an air of lavender and old lace. Her jibes, more often than not, seem to be made over the hint of a smile — real malice does not seem to be a part of her nature. She turns to HELENA.)* Are we out of order?

HELENA. It would appear so.

EVIE. Then you'd better get on with it, young man, hadn't you?

BILL. I'm just waiting on me mate.

EVIE. I see. And where might your mate be?

BILL. *(nodding towards the garden)* He's coming now.

EVIE. *(to HELENA:)* No paper this morning? No post?

HELENA. Oh, I'm sorry. *(She starts to wipe her hands.)*

EVIE. No coffee?

HELENA. I'll do it now.

EVIE. Good. Better late than never. *(HELENA starts to go, giving BILL a hard look in passing.)*

BILL. Well don't look at me. *(at her retreating back)* It was a beautiful day. *(HELENA has gone.)*

EVIE. It still is by the looks of it. Helena being crotchety again?

BILL. You might say she's been getting up my nose a bit.

EVIE. Might I?

BILL. Took what might be called an instant dislike I guess.

EVIE. Do you? Well, I wouldn't worry about it.

BILL. Oh I ain't worried.

EVIE. It's just her manner. *(HELENA returns to hand over the morning paper, neatly folded.)*

EVIE. Ah ... thank you, my dear.

HELENA. I'll get the coffee.

EVIE. Young man, I take it you and your mate might care for a cup of coffee?

BILL. I wouldn't say no.

EVIE. Then don't.

BILL. Ta. *(EVIE nods to HELENA who, with another hard look at BILL, goes.)* She's not likely to put anything in it, is she? *(EVIE raises an eyebrow.)* Only kidding.

EVIE. I do love my morning cup of coffee. Well, let's see what horrible events have taken place in the world since last night's news.

BILL. There's been another plane hi-jacked. Heard it on the radio this morning.

EVIE. *(looking at the paper)* Yes. More revolutionaries?

BILL. Terrible that is. Christ! ... I beg your pardon. But it makes me really ... you know ... *(He holds both hands out in front of him, palms upwards, fingers bent, searching for words.)* ...I mean, well what about all the passengers then? I mean, you get a dozen crazy punters with guns and hand grenades and that, and all those people sitting in there ... Can you think what it must be like? Torture. That's what it is an' all. Sheer bloody torture. And what have they done? Gone for a ride in an aero-plane. That's all. I dunno. Just going about their own business an' that 'appens.

EVIE. What would you do with them?

BILL. Me? You mean, the hi-jackers?

EVIE. Yes. What would you do with them? Tell me. I would be interested to hear your views.

BILL. String'em up by the ... String'em up. every man jack of'em. Ladies too. Strikes me they're worse than the men when it comes to it. Or put 'em up against a wall. Shoot the bastards. Shoot 'em and be done with it.

EVIE. But what if they have a cause? That about their ideals? Their aspirations?

BILL. That to their aspirations! *(making a finger)* They got no right getting innocent people into that predicament, not for anything. And anyone who says they has needs to have his head examined.

EVIE. Well ... where will it all end?

BILL. Put a stop to their bloody nonsense. I mean, that's piracy that is. They used to hang people for piracy on the high seas. What about the high air?

EVIE. And what about the muggings? And the bombings?

The assassinations. The kidnappings. Look, there's been another, in Italy. Kidnapping.

BILL. Oh well, what do you expect? Italy! Huh.

EVIE. Five-year-old daughter of a business tycoon, snatched right from under her mother's nose. Oh, dear.

BILL. Bloody mafia.

EVIE. Well, it's our own fault I suppose.

BILL. How do you mean?

EVIE. It's the world we've created isn't it? There isn't any kind of respect for law and order any more, for people, their property, their rights, no pride in achievement. It's all get, these days. Get, get get.

(DELL Enters from the garden. He is a young man of about twenty-three, handsome in a flash sort of way. He is sporting a large rose in his lapel and carries a canvas holdall.)

BILL. Took your time didn't you?

DELL. Hey, how do you like my...? *(He sees EVIE looking at him.)* Oh ... beg your pardon.

EVIE. Young man, do you usually go through people's gardens pinching their prize roses?

DELL. What? Oh ... this?

EVIE. That.

DELL. Oh, well ... *(He looks at BILL.)*

EVIE. It's been a good year for roses. They should really have been fnished by now but, with the extended warm days, there's still quite a few about.

DELL. *(matter of fact)* I'm sorry.

EVIE. And so you should be. Do you know the story of

beauty and the beast? *(DELL shakes his head.)* Well, fortunately for you, there's no beast here to make you pay for your vandalism.

BILL. You'll have to excuse him, missus.

EVIE. Will I?

BILL. He's got no idea, he really hasn't. Like all the modern generation. Come on you, let's get cracking.

DELL. What you on about? Modern generation.

BILL. Worse than a ruddy football holligan you are. Come on.

EVIE. *(eyeing the holdall)* I hope you've brought the right tools.

BILL. What kind of tools ought I to have?

EVIE. People who arrive to do repairs seldom seem to have the right tools. They invariably have to go away and come back. Only they don't come back. Somebody else comes.

BILL. You're getting us mixed up with the Gas Board again. I keep telling you.

EVIE. You keep telling me what?

BILL. Oh no. It was her, that's right.

EVIE. They either have the wrong tools or the wrong parts.

BILL. Have no fear, missus. I've got all I need for this little job and, once it's done, that's the last you'll see of us. We won't be back.

EVIE. That is most reassuring.

BILL. Right then, if someone'll show us where the extensions are, we'll be getting on with it.

EVIE. John will show you. *(She picks up a small hand bell and rings it, then goes back to her paper.)* Corruption in high places doesn't help of course, or set any kind of example. It's little wonder the youth of today are so confused. *(DELL looks at BILL — "What's she on about?" BILL shrugs.)* With no one to give them a lead, set them any standards. Look at the politicians today: dishonest, hypocritical, half-baked charlatans. Or woolly headed idealists who wouldn't know reality if it were a brick in the face from a football hooligan who steals roses from old ladies. When last did we have a real statesman? A real leader.

BILL. Well, all I can say is, consider yourself lucky, lady. I mean, stuck out here in the middle of nowhere, in a nice, peaceful, quiet place like this. Fine house, almost a palace you might say, with your beautiful roses. You can sit back and let them all get on with it, can't you? I mean, why should you worry?

EVIE. Why? I'm still in the world, aren't I? Such as it is.

BILL. It's not such a bad old place really.

EVIE. In my opinion it gets worse day by day.

BILL. Worse or better depends on your point of view dunnit?

EVIE. Nobody in their proper mind could possibly take the view that the decadence we see all around us is an improvement.

BILL. And that depends on what you mean by decadence.

DELL. Yeh. *(EVIE and BILL stare at DELL.)* And what you mean by improvement. I mean, improvement on what? I mean, ten years ago? Fifteen? Fifty? Victorian times? Well, I'm here to tell you, missus, I like the times we live in. I reckon them to be a great improvement on anything that went before. Oh, I give you, they're dangerous. But, exciting. You know what I mean?

EVIE. Obviously you don't travel much in aeroplanes.

(JOHN appears in the doorway. His cheek is covered with a band-aid.)

EVIE. Ah, John ... Good God, man! What have you done to your face?

JOHN. An accident, madam.

EVIE. I do wish you'd give up that old-fashioned razor and use a modern safety one.

BILL. Well, there you are. Razor's an improvement, anyway.

EVIE. I've never known anyone to cut himself with such monotonous regularity. John, be so kind as to give these two gentlemen a guided tour of our telephone system. *(to DELL as he passes her:)* Do you really appreciate that? Or did you pick it merely because it was there ... like people climb mountains?

BILL. Oh, he'd really like to appreciate the good things in life. Wouldn't you? But he's never really had a chance, you see. And, until he met me, you know, he never knew what he really wanted. Did you? Hey? *(He gives DELL a playful tap on the arm.)*

DELL. That's right.

JOHN. This way, if you please.

BILL. Right behind you, guv.

(JOHN goes out followed by BILL and DELL. EVIE crosses to the garden door and looks out. PETERS is passing by.)

EVIE. Ah, Peters...

PETERS. *(off)* Good morning, madam.

EVIE. I take it Miss Keeley gave you my message.

PETERS. She did. And I'll see to it.

EVIE. I should have given you orders to stand guard over the roses but it's a bit late for that now. *(shaking her head)* It would be impossible to mount a permanent guard over everything anyway. *(She turns back to the room.)* Isn't there a warning in the Bible somewhere about thieves in the night? I hope his light fingers stray no further than the rose bushes. I'd better have a word with John.

(HELENA Enters with a tray: coffee, milk, sugar, cups and saucers.)

EVIE. Ah, coffee ... No sign of them yet?

HELENA. No.

EVIE. Business trips! Always business trips. Why doesn't that man take a real holiday for a change?

HELENA. Maybe he feels that in the present economic climate...

EVIE. MISS Helena Keeley! If you must open your mouth to make what passes for conversation, kindly also make some endeavor, no matter how difficult it might be for you, not to be completely idiotic. You know nothing whatsoever about my nephew-in-law, and even less about the supposed economic climate.

HELENA. I'm sorry.

EVIE. And don't add insult to injury by whining.

HELENA. Well, at least it will be a holiday for her.

Evie. Will it?

Helena. I thought that was the intention.

Evie. There you are, you see. You're at it again. Expressing an opinion with no knowledge of the facts. The intention is for my nephew-in-law to save himself having to give his wife a proper holiday at all. What's she going to do with herself with him attending conferences all day and every day?

Helena. Well at least they'll have a couple of days in London before they go. And, if he's at conferences all day, that'll give her plenty of time to see the sights.

Evie. On her own? She'll come back with her bottom black and blue.

Helena. I thought the Italian government had brought in a law about ... pinching bottoms. Foreign ones, anyway.

Evie. I'm sure that only makes it much more exciting. He who pinches and runs away lives to pinch another day.

Helena. I'll give the workmen their coffee.

Evie. Workmen? They're not workmen. Not any more. The working classes don't like to be called that anymore, you know, unless it's for propaganda purposes. They're not simply telephone engineers. In accordance with the madness of the modern world they probably have some ultra-fancy title, like ... Audio aid communications system restoration operatives.

Helena. Whatever they call themselves, they still want their coffee. Is there such a thing as a *nephew*-in-law?

Evie. Well, he married the Colonel's niece, so what else could he be?

(HELENA is about to go when there is the sound of a MOTOR HORN, DOGS BARKING.)

HELENA. Oh! They're here! They're here! *(In her excitement, she slops the coffee.)*

EVIE. Now don't panic so, Helena. Why do you get so excited? Good heavens, you're worse than the wretched dogs. Just calm down and fetch two more coffee cups.

HELENA. Yes. I'm sorry.

EVIE. And do stop apologizing.

HELENA. It's just that I've so looked forward to David being here.

EVIE. And stop justifying yourself. *(HELENA goes through the house followed by EVIE, her voice growing fainter as she goes.)* I'm really beginning to think you're incurable, Helena. There is absolutely no hope for you. Sometimes I wonder why I put up with you at all. The Colonel certainly wouldn't have. Not for a moment. But then, if he were alive, you wouldn't be here anyway, would you?

(BILL appears from the side of the conservatory. He is holding the canvas holdall. He stands looking in the direction in which the two women have gone. JOHN follows him.)

JOHN. This way.

BILL. *(turning to him)* Hmm?

(JOHN indicates the stairs. BILL nods and follows him. As they go there is the sound of voices returning presumably coming in through the front door.)

EVIE. *(off)* Nonsense! Of course you've got time. You'll stay long enough for a cup of coffee. That's the least we'd expect. Now, young man, into the kitchen and Helena will see to you. She's been looking forward to this for weeks. And, when he's had his refreshment, straight up to the nursery with him. *(Appears in the doorway. she pauses to look back.)* Come along, you two, we're in the conservatory.

(She moves down to the table as ROLAND and PENNY follow to the door. PENNY is in her early thirties, ROLAND is a little older.)

EVIE. Now then ... Oh, dear ... cups. I did tell Helena...

PENNY. I'll get them.

EVIE. *(going back to the door)* Not at all. You sit right down there and relax. I won't be a sec. *(EVEIE disappears, leaving ROLAND and PENNY in the doorway. ROLAND looks at his watch. PENNY waggles a finger in front of his nose.)*

PENNY. Uh-huh.

ROLAND. Well...

PENNY. You heard the order, Mr. Thompson. You'll stay long enough for a cup of coffee.

ROLAND. One cup of coffee can take a long time.

PENNY. *(putting her arms about his neck)* Now please, darling. Try to relax? For my sake, just make the effort.

ROLAND. One cannot relax at the same time as making an effort. It is a direct contradiction.

PENNY. What happened to that much vaunted, lateral thinking you're always on about? Making an effort to relax seems perfectly logical to me.

ROLAND. Female logic.

PENNY. Male chauvinism. *(She kisses him lightly.)* Now, please! Just for me? Why does it always have to be such an ordeal?

ROLAND. She makes me uncomfortable.

PENNY. Evie? Makes you uncomfortable? But why? That's ridiculous.

ROLAND. *(He shrugs.)* Ridiculous it may be, but true nevertheless. And this place ... it's a mausoleum.

PENNY. Roland! It's beauitful!

ROLAND. Penny ... it is hideous.

PENNY. You've never said that before.

ROLAND. Doesn't mean I never thought it.

PENNY. No, I won't have it. Not everyone, you know, considers your plastic laminate world to be the ultimate in aesthetic living.

ROLAND. And you've never said that before.

PENNY. Yes I have. You just haven't heard.

ROLAND. Penny, there are things from the past which are beauitful, there are some things which are not, and this isn't. It's a folly. A huge, grotesque piece of Victorian extravagance, built to prove what a bright boy the Colonel's grandfather was to make so much money out of the railways. That's all.

PENNY. All right, I'm not going to argue. To me it is beautiful. And this ... *(indicating the conservatory)* ... this is the most beautiful part of it. My magic place.

ROLAND. *(laughing)* And what does that mean?

PENNY. Ah, you see? There are things I haven't told you either.

ROLAND. Tell me then.

PENNY. Well, when I was a little girl, this is where I was always happiest, so it became my magic place. That's what I called it. *(ROLAND stares at her.)* I don't suppose little boys have magic places. *(ROLAND looks around the conservatory, then sits on the sofa. PENNY laughs.)* Oh, Roland, if you could see your face. You're so ... English! Am I embarrassing you?

ROLAND. Not at all.

PENNY. *(She joins him on the sofa, pushing him back.)* What would you do...? Supposing, one hot summer night, I suggested we strip off and make love on the village cricket pitch, would that be the ultimate sacrilege?

ROLAND. You're in one of your nonsense moods.

PENNY. Would you divorce me? Or merely bite your stiff upper lip and consider me eccentric? Or would England finally fall apart and sink beneath the waves?

ROLAND. *(He gets out from beneath her and moves away.)* Where do you get these ideas from? In the first place it would be bloody uncomfortable and in the second place, for your information, I don't think of myself as being particularly Enlgish.

PENNY. How do you think of yourself?

ROLAND. As a European, of course.

PENNY. Never!

ROLAND. *(looking at his watch)* Darling, I really mean it, we mustn't stay too long.

PENNY. There you are.

ROLAND. There you are what?

PENNY. You're about as European as fish and chips in Torremolinos.

ROLAND. Now how do you arrive at that conclusion from my keeping a watch on the time?

PENNY. *(Shrugs.)* Do you really not like this house? That makes me rather sad.

ROLAND. Oh, I just don't find it comfortable, that's all.

PENNY. What could possibly make you feel uncomfortable in this old house...?

ROLAND. It's spooky.

PENNY. That's the very last thing it is, spooky. Not for me anyway. It's full of memories, Roland, and they're all beautiful ones, especially in here. I used to creep down here at night sometimes, after everyone had gone to bed, and see the moon shining down through the roof. And the plants would come alive. You could hear them, whispering.

ROLAND. I told you ... spooky.

PENNY. And out there, in the black shadows, wild animals prowled, huge shaggy wolves with great yellow eyes and bared fangs.

ROLAND. There you are, you must have scared yourself half to death.

PENNY. No! In here you were perfectly safe.

ROLAND. With plants talking to each other!

PENNY. Roland, didn't you ever have fantasies as a child?

(EVIE Enters with two more cups and saucers.)

EVIE. Of course he did. He still does. But, whenever they raise their beautiful heads ... *(She pats his cheek.)* ... he flattens them with his deposit book.

PENNY. Oh, Evie! I don't know how, or why, you got it into your tiny little head that Roland is a Scrooge.

EVIE. Well, why doesn't he feed his child, for a start?

ROLAND. What do you mean by that? *(EVIE starts to pour the coffee.)*

EVIE. He's tucking into slab cake as if it were delivered in ten ton trucks.

PENNY. Evie! Helena's not going to spoil him, is she?

EVIE. Of course she is. What else does a plain spinster do with a child she dotes on? *(PENNY looks at ROLAND.)*

EVIE. Oh, don't worry. I'll keep my beady little eye on them. Now then, black for Roland, lots of milk for Penny, and in-between for me. *(She hands them their coffee.)* I've told Helena to take David up to the nursery as soon as he's had his fill. He's probably tired out with excitement and the journey.

ROLAND. Do you know what that child put away for breakfast? Enough to satisfy a regiment.

EVIE. I was only joking, Roland. Though, if an army marches on its stomach, yours wouldn't make it to the barrack gates before dropping dead from malnutrition. Do sit down and relax, dear.

ROLAND. We mustn't stay too long, Evie.

EVIE. And stop repeating yourself. For heaven's sake, I haven't seen you for months and months, you can spare me five minutes. How many ulcers has he got now?

PENNY. None ... that I know of.

EVIE. Well how far is he off a coronary then?

(HELENA appears in the doorway.)

HELENA. David wants to go out in the garden and play with the dogs.

EVIE. Well, he can't. He will do as he is told and go up to the nursery. And he won't take the dogs up there with him either. *(HELENA gives EVIE a hard look and goes. To PENNY:)* There, see how forceful I can be? Now, let's start with Roland's favorite, one and only topic of conversation. How's business?

ROLAND. Lousy.

EVIE. Well I AM sorry to hear that. Would you like a loan?

ROLAND. It's not that lousy.

EVIE. You mean, even if you wanted a loan, you wouldn't ask me for it. That's very unkind.

PENNY. Now stop it, you two. I never know when to take you seriously.

EVIE. Oh, don't take him seriously at all. Business is far from lousy. Quite the contrary. The company made a pretax profit of just under a million for the half year and your husband has recommended a rise in dividend of twelve and a half percent.

ROLAND. Aren't you pleased?

EVIE. Of course I am. Not half so pleased as the tax man, though. Most of it will go to him.

ROLAND. Anyway, it's gratifying to note that you do, at least, read the chairman's report.

EVIE. Not all of it. Only the salient points. Your

speeches really are very dull, Roland. Why don't you put some pep into them? Jazz them up a little.

ROLAND. Entertainment is not what the exercise is all about. What do you want me to do? Come on at the head of a row of chorus girls? *(PENNY laughs. ROLAND glances at her, then back to EVIE.)*

EVIE. What a splendid idea. And we now know where your fantasies lie.

ROLAND. I put my "pep" into the business, which is why it is successful and which is why you are worth what you are.

EVIE. Roland, how kind. Are you really doing it all for me? Now don't glower like that. *(to PENNY:)* Your husband has no sense of humor, dear. Can't think why you married him.

PENNY. There are qualities in a husband other than a sense of humor.

EVIE. Hmph! Well, that little foray having opened the meeting, we'll skip standing orders and go on to any other business. Are you excited? *(PENNY looks a little puzzled.)* About your holiday, dear. You are going on holiday ... *(at ROLAND)* ... aren't you?

PENNY. Yes, I am.

EVIE. Am what? Excited? Or going on holiday?

PENNY. Both. I'm excited about going on holiday.

EVIE. Well you're hiding your enthusiasm with remarkable aplomb. Don't look at your watch, Roland. And don't say you have to be going. You haven't finished your coffee.

ROLAND. And I wasn't looking at my watch.

EVIE. Only because I anticipated. *(ROLAND looks at his watch.)*

EVIE. Does he ever look at you like that?

PENNY. Evie, you are determined that Roland and I will leave here and start a fight the minute we get in the car.

EVIE. How could you say such a thing?

PENNY. You are determined that he will say all sorts of wicked things about you.

EVIE. *(impishly)* Truthful wicked things.

PENNY. Then I will feel obliged, duty bound, to defend you, and the argument will continue all the way down the M1. Well I'm sorry to have to disappoint you but it isn't going to happen.

EVIE. Of course it isn't. Because Roland knows I'm only teasing. Don't you, dear? And he's not going to be so silly as to start a row on the eve of your wonderful adventure together. Oh, you'll have such a lovely time in Rome. Just the two of you. Like a second honeymoon. You did have a first honeymoon, didn't you? *(Seeing PENNY'S face, EVIE laughs and raises both hands, placating.)* All right, all right. I'll stop teasing. Though I think it very mean of you, not allowing a harmless old lady her fun.

ROLAND. *(laughing)* Evie, you are about as harmless as a black widow spider.

EVIE. Oh, Roland, you're so obvious. you have absolutely no finesse. I knew you were thinking it so why did you have to spoil it by saying it?

ROLAND. And I've finished my coffee.

EVIE. And you've scalded your tongue, which serves you right. *(to PENNY:)* Do I dare suggest you might like to look 'round the gardens before you're dragged away?

PENNY. Do you mind if I left that for the return journey?

EVIE. Of course I mind. Not that it would make any difference. *(She gets up and heads for the garden door.)* So why don't we compromise and make our way to the car this way?

PENNY. Should we look in on David before we go?

ROLAND. *(Shakes his head.)* And, Evie, when I walk out of that door, I'm heading straight for the car. Is that understood? I am not, repeat, NOT going to make a detour via the roses, the shrubberies, the lily ponds and the kitchen gardens. Do I make myself absolutely clear?

EVIE. Absolutely, dear. *(She takes his arm.)* Isn't it nice that we understand each other so well? I'm so glad you married Penny. She might not be my daughter, but I've always thought of her as such.

(They go out. For a moment the conservatory is empty. The LIGHTS change. There are CHILD NOISES, possibily a nursery rhyme record or maybe the jingle of a MUSIC BOX. Throughout the play this device is used, instead of tabs, for scene changes and time lapses. JOHN Enters from the side of the conservatory as LIGHTS come up and CHILD NOISES fade. He crosses over to look out of the garden door, then turns back to survey the conservatory. His glance takes in EVIE'S locked cupboard. He goes over to it and inspects the lock, looks around again, goes back to HELENA'S bench and takes up the pruning knife. He starts off for the cupboard again but decides he needs some cover, so he turns back to pick up the coffee tray, placing the knife on it. HELENA Enters through the main door just as JOHN turns back with the

tray. He gives a guilty start, almost dropping the tray, and hurriedly puts it down. He leans on the bench, his back to HELENA as she advances jauntily towards him. He suddenly swings around knife in hand, and lashes out at her. She screams and leaps back. JOHN, obviously furious, advances on her.)

HELENA. What are you doing?

JOHN. You want a little game of tit for tat? Huh?

HELENA. Stop it! Stop it! Don't. Put it down, please!

(With relief, she sees EVIE approaching and JOHN guesses at her presence by HELENA'S reaction. He brushes angrily past her and into the house. HELENA goes over to the bench, selects a vase and starts to arrange the flowers. There is a moment and then EVIE Re-enters from the garden.)

EVIE. Well, there you are then, safely on their way. How's the child?

HELENA. Sleeping like an angel.

EVIE. You can, of course, personally vouch for the way angels sleep. *(EVIE sits down and picks up her paper.)*

HELENA. *(still obviously upset)* It was nice to see Mr. and Mrs. Thompson again, even if it was such a brief visit. Did they enjoy the garden?

EVIE. Of course. Roland was amazed by the roses, delighted by the shrubberies, fascinated by the lily ponds, enthralled with the kitchen garden and is probably at this moment swearing blue murder all the way down the M1. *(She chuckles to herself.)* Well why shouldn't they afford an old lady half an hour of their precious time? Is that too much to ask? Pity they couldn't stay for lunch. What is for lunch anyway?

(BILL Enters from the house, carrying his holdall.)

EVIE. Oh, you're still here, are you? Having trouble?

BILL. No, no trouble. No trouble at all. What had to be done has been done. You will be pleased to hear that you are no longer incommunicado.

EVIE. Thank you. And where is your light-fingered friend? Not in the dining room, I hope, nicking my best silver. Is that the right expression?

BILL. It could be the right expression but, no, as a matter of fact, he's sitting in the van waiting for me.

EVIE. Well, if anything's gone missing, the first call I shall make on my newly repaired telephone will be a nine, nine, nine.

BILL. *(making for the door)* Your privilege, me old darling.

EVIE. And, for your information, young man, I do not consider myself to be your old darling.

BILL. That's all right, me old darling. You can be sarky, I can be sarky. Maybe you'd like to take a butchers through me holdall before I go.

EVIE. I would like to what?

BILL. Take a butchers. *(no response)* Butchers! *(EVIE looks at HELENA, back to BILL)* Where've you been all your life? Don't you know what a butchers is?

EVIE. It's a place where they deal in meat.

BILL. No! It means "look," take a look. It's rhyming slang, see? "Butcher's hook" — "Look."

EVIE. What a curious expression.

BILL. Apples and pears — stairs. Plates of meat — feet. Now come on, what's "me old china?"

EVIE. I haven't the faintest idea.

BILL. That's me mate, in'it? China plate — mate. (*BILL grins, looking from one stony face to the other. Finally EVIE breaks the silence.*)

EVIE. Collar!

BILL. What?

EVIE. Collar.

BILL. (*shrugging*) Never heard that before.

EVIE. Don't you get it? (*BILL shakes his head.*) Collar and stud? Stud! (*BILL still looks puzzled.*) Blood.

BILL. Well there IS a curious expression for you. What makes a nice old lady like you think of something like that? Tch, I dunno. Anyway, I was thinking of tie, collar and tie. I couldn't work out what rhymes with tie.

EVIE. There doesn't seem to be any logic in it and that just came into my head. I thought it was quite clever. I'll think of some more.

BILL. Yeh, well while you're thinking, I'll be off.

EVIE. Here's one for you — marrow.

BILL. Marrow?

EVIE. Yes, come on. You should get that one.

BILL. What have I started?

EVIE. Do you want a clue? Thank you for mending my marrow.

BILL. Hey?

EVIE. Telephone!

BILL. How'd you get that from marrow?

EVIE. Marrow and bone — phone.

BILL. That's macabre, that is. Who would have thought of that?

EVIE. I did.

BILL. Well, for your information, it's "*Dog* and Bone."

EVIE. Is it? Come on, Helena, now you think of one.

HELENA. I don't think...

BILL. Yes. Well, look, ladies, while you're playing your little game, I'll scarper, okay? I got a load of work on. Nice to have met you. Thanks for the coffee and tara then. *(Goes out through the garden door, whistling as he goes.)*

EVIE. Do you think I upset him?

HELENA. Why should you have upset him? And, if you did, I can't see that it matters, not after the way he spoke to you. In fact, I would report him to his superiors.

EVIE. He doesn't have any superiors. There aren't any superiors anymore. By the way, did you see the young one go out?

HELENA. No. Why?

EVIE. It doesn't matter. *(Goes back to her paper.)*

(There is the sound of a MOTOR starting up and van driving away.)

HELENA. *(Stands back from her flower arrangement and admires it.)* There ... how's that?

EVIE. *(looking up)* Well, it's hardly a classic example of ikebana or Constance Spry, but it will pass.

HELENA. They never seem to want to stay where I put

them. *(She gives a stem a half-hearted twist but it immediately falls back to where it was.)*

EVIE. Pretend you meant it to be like that. Aren't you using one of those sharp, spiky things?

HELENA. A pin holder? I haven't got one to fit in this vase. *(She opens a cupboard door and takes out two pin holders. One is real, the other is the fake which will be used later for the attack on BILL. She takes both pin holders over to the bench and puts the fake one down, keeping the other in her hand until, with a little cry of pain, she drops it and clutches her finger.)*

EVIE. Did you catch yourself? They're meant to be picked up by the base, you know, not the spikes.

HELENA. *(examining her finger)* They're so sharp!

EVIE. Of course. Like sharks' teeth. Have you ever felt a shark's tooth? I have. That must be the reddest tooth in nature. *(HELENA wraps her handkerchief around a finger — she is the kind of girl who would have more than one handkerchief.)* I wonder what the reddest claw is. Does that need a band-aid?

HELENA. I don't think so. It will probably stop in a minute.

EVIE. Everyone's very busy mutilating themselves this morning. You really ought to be more careful. They say that ninety-eight percent of accidents happen in the home. This place will end up looking like a battlefield or a Red Cross emergency post. I suppose the tiger is reddest in claw. They say a tiger eats as it kills. The lion kills before it eats but the tiger actually eats as it's killing.

HELENA. Cats are cruel.

EVIE. Cats?

HELENA. *(She removes the handkerchief to look at her finger, then puts it back.)* The way they torment their victims.

EVIE. Only to our way of thinking. I hardly think a cat looks on its prey as a victim. Now the really vicious animal is the African buffalo.

HELENA. How do you know that?

EVIE. Well ... *(story time)* ... the Colonel told me, when he was on safari in Africa ... I forget where it was exactly, but I've seen pictures. Flat country, very dry and dotted with thorny trees. He was warned that, of all the wild animals, the one to be feared most was the African buffalo. You wouldn't think so, would you? To look at it, placid as an ox. But, evidently, it is the most vicious, the most spiteful, the most evil-tempered, the most stubborn beast in the world.

HELENA. I'm not so sure I recall what an African buffalo looks like.

EVIE. The Colonel was told this story about a white hunter who was trapped by a buffalo. He hadn't shot the animal. It wasn't wounded and maddened with pain or anything like that. No, it just decided it didn't like him and it trapped him in one of the thorn trees. He'd lost his gun and his horse was standing tethered nearby. Maybe he'd stopped for a drink at a water hole or something. I don't remember the exact details. Yes, I think that was it. Anyway, the buffalo tried to get him out of the tree by charging and shaking and, when that didn't work, the creature, now in an absolute fury of frustration, turned its attention to the horse. Well, by the time the buffalo had finished with the horse, there was very little of that animal left. The man had to watch from the tree while the buffalo gored and gouged, tore, trampled, kicked, kneaded, rolled and tossed fragments of horse in all directions. Then, absolutely exhausted, it lay down close to the tree. Night fell. And, in the morning, the buffalo was still there. It tried again to shake the man out of the tree. The man slipped and one leg got trapped in a fork, just low enough for the buffalo's horn to hook into his boot. Well, when the man's friends evenutally arrived on the scene, they found the buffalo, covered in blood, lying beneath the tree and the man still dangling above. He had no foot. From the calf down there was just bones and tendon. *(HELENA sits abruptly in the nearest chair.)* You know how rough a cat's tongue is? Well, a buffalo's tongue is like a rasp and the animal found that by standing up on its hind legs it could reach the man's foot with its tongue. It found it could lick the man's foot down to the bone, and that's exactly what it did.

HELENA. That's the most horrible story I've ever heard.

EVIE. The colonel was full of stories about his days in Africa. He was a marvelous raconteur, the life and soul of any dinner party.

HELENA. I hope he didn't tell stories like that! *(EVIE looks at her.)* Well, it would certainly have put me off my food.

EVIE. You're too squeamish for your own good, Miss Keeley. And speaking of food, you didn't tell me what's for lunch.

HELENA. I believe it's Konigsburger Klopse. At least I think that's what John said.

EVIE. Oh, good.

HELENA. Is there anything you want me to do for you

before lunch?

EVIE. *(going back to her paper)* No thank you.

HELENA. I'll take these through then. *(She gets up and goes back to her vase of flowers.)*

EVIE. And after Konigsburger Klopse ... apfelkuchn. Ah, as a girl I spent so many happy ... I had so many happy times in Germany. My father was in the diplomatic corps you know. I was very fond of my father. A splendid man. Very strict, of course, but a wonderful man. What does your father do?

HELENA. Oh, he was in banking. *(deciding to be honest)* He was a bank clerk. I've lost both my parents.

EVIE. No family? No brothers or sisters? *(HELENA shakes her head.)*

HELENA. I don't think Mummy and Daddy were very suited to each other. Or very happy.

EVIE. We've never really had a chance to discuss each other, have we?

HELENA. No, we haven't. Not really.

EVIE. Or maybe it's been a lack of inclination. Funny. How lives come together. Don't you think?

HELENA. How do you mean?

EVIE. The effect we have on each other. I don't mean you and I specifically, I mean people in general. Do you believe, for example, that the murderer selects his victim? Or does the victim select his killer? Or do you think it's a reciprocal arrangement? Or fate? Sheer chance? *(HELENA is uncomfortable and out of her depth. She pretends to be thinking hard.)* And why do people marry the people they do?

HELENA. *(happier with this)* Oh, there must be a

million reasons.

EVIE. There are also a million other people they could marry just as easily.

HELENA. I suppose so.

EVIE. But you don't believe it. You still believe in Mr. Right, do you?

HELENA. You met the Colonel ... quite late in life, didn't you?

EVIE. You mean there's hope for you, yet? Well, there's not much hope sitting out here, living vicariously through the pages of romantic novels and playing companion to an old lady. You'll die an old maid. I'm not trying to be unkind. I'm giving you advice. You don't have to be like the buffalo and actually tree your man, but at least you have to be in the right hunting grounds. Don't you like men?

HELENA. Of course I do. I just haven't much experience of them.

EVIE. And you're not likely to have at this rate. I ought to be kind and fire you.

HELENA. The Colonel, from his photographs, he seemed a fine figure of a man.

EVIE. He was.

HELENA. Was it the war that brought you together?

EVIE. Indeed it was. Indeed it was.

HELENA. Was it very romantic?

EVIE. *(suddenly harsh)* No, it wasn't at all romantic. But it was eminently practical.

(The TELEPHONE rings. It rings a couple of times before HELENA goes to answer it.)

HELENA. Hel... *(to EVIE:)* It's a callbox! Hello? ... I beg your pardon?

EVIE. Who is it?

HELENA. *(covering the mouthpiece and covering up the fact that she recognizes the voice)* It's a man. He ... *(into phone)* Look, who is this please? *(Covers mouthpiece.)* It's a man. He says it's very important. He wants to talk to the old lady.

EVIE. Old lady!

HELENA. I'm sorry, Mrs. Webster is not available at the moment and, unless you tell me who ... *(Covers mouthpiece, then says reluctantly.)* ... He says, it's your old china.

EVIE. Oh, it's HIM, is it? What on earth can he want? Tell him I'm busy.

HELENA. I'm sorry, Mrs. Webster is busy right at this moment. *(There is a silence and then HELENA again covers the mouthpiece and looks at EVIE. She is trembling and can hardly find her voice.)* He says, when you've got a moment, from being busy ... take a look in the nursery. *(Silence. Then EVIE gets to her feet and crosses to the phone, taking it from HELENA.)*

EVIE. Yes? *(to HELENA:)* He's rung off. *(She puts down the phone.)* Go and take a look in the nursery.

HELENA. No!

EVIE. Do as I say. Be quick about it, woman. Go on! *(HELENA runs into the house and up the stairs.)*

(EVIE waits. Again the LIGHTS change and we hear the CHILD SOUNDS. This holds for about fifteen seconds and then the sound of the TELEPHONE cuts across it and the LIGHTS immediately change back.)

HELENA. *(Comes down the stairs.)* He's not there! He's not there! *(EVIE reaches for the phone.)* Maybe he's gone outside.

EVIE. Be quiet. *(She lifts the receiver.)* (You there, me old darling.) Yes, I'm here ... (Have you taken a butcher's?) ... Yes, we've taken a butcher's ... (Do you suppose there'd be a reward for the missing goods?) ...How much? ... (Well, I don't want to be too greedy, but there's Dell to think of, isn't there? All those good things in life he's missed out on. Say, er ... fifty thousand?) ... I see ... (Good. You agree on the price, then?) ... Are you making me responsible? ... (I don't care who pays up. You or his dad, so long as we're paid.) ... I shouldn't think his father could raise that much that quickly. I don't know whether I can contact him ... (Well, whether you can or not, all you have to do is get the money and leave it in the greenhouse in the kitchen garden. You have forty eight hours. Failure to comply with these instructions means you won't see the goods again. Okay, me old darling? And there's no need for me to tell you not to do anything silly, is there? Like, thinking of going to the police? Tara, then.) *(EVIE puts down the phone. HELENA is standing, staring at her, open-mouthed.)* Telephone engineers. *(She shakes her head and moves slowly back into the conservatory.)* Miss Keeley, would you be so kind as to fetch the brandy and two glasses, please?

HELENA. I ... I...

EVIE. Don't stand there opening and shutting your mouth like a particularly repulsive fish. Just do as I say. *(HELENA goes quickly. EVIE moves to the table and sits down, staring straight ahead. HELENA returns with a decanter and two glasses which she puts on the table.)* Pour. *(HELENA does so, her hand shaking, slopping brandy on the table. EVIE lifts her glass.)* Thank you. *(EVIE sips her brandy. HELENA knocks hers back and chokes. EVIE waits for the fit of whooping cough to subside. Very shakily, HELENA sits down.)* Better?

HELENA. *(Nods.)* What did the man say?

EVIE. What I expected him to say. They have kidnapped the child. They want fifty thousand pounds. It is to be left in the greenhouse in the kitchen garden. The time limit is forty eight hours. If we don't comply with these instructions, as he so quaintly put it, we will not see the goods again.

HELENA. Oh, my God! What are we going to do?

EVIE. We are going to think.

HELENA. Aren't you going to call the police? *(EVIE turns to give her a withering look and then looks out front again.)* But you must!

EVIE. I must do nothing of the kind. If I do, the child is as good as dead.

HELENA. And if you don't? *(EVIE sits staring straight ahead, thinking.)* But you must do something. *(silence)* Are you going to pay? *(silence)* Penny and Roland! I'm going to call the police.

EVIE. That's what he meant.

HELENA. What?

EVIE. When he said, "What had to be done has been done." That's what he meant.

HELENA. How could they have got David out of the house?

EVIE. There are any number of doors.

HELENA. But you could see the van from here, where it was parked.

EVIE. There was nobody this side of the house when he was taken out. He was so sure of himself, standing here, talking about apples and pears. Where do you suppose he made that call from? Somewhere close by. They couldn't have gone very far. They haven't been gone much more than five minutes. *(HELENA starts to cry.)* Pull yourself together, Helena, you're not helping the situation. If it comes to it, the ransom will be paid and the boy returned safe and sound. In the meantime ... *(She pushes the decanter towards HELENA.)* ... try not to go to pieces.

HELENA. How can you be so calm about it?

EVIE. I'm thinking. Now, where did he make that call from?

HELENA. The phone-box in Natalie's Lane. That would be the nearest. That's about five minutes away in the car.

EVIE. Yes, that could be. Now here's a question for you to answer. Why would he call from there? *(HELENA looks blank.)* What I mean is, it's virtually on the doorstep, so why call from there? Why not call from twenty miles away? Forty? Fifty! Why not put time and distance between us and them? Wouldn't that be more usual?

HELENA. *(wailing)* I don't know I don't know! Please ... Why don't you just call the police?

EVIE. No! That was a stupid thing to do. Stupid and dangerous.

HELENA. What?

EVIE. Calling from so close. Unless of course it was necessary to the plan.

HELENA. What plan?

EVIE. *(snapping)* Oh, Helena! If you can't help me then go to your room. No! On second thoughts stay right where you are. I'm not having you sneaking to the telephone behind my back and calling up the local constabulary. There's something very strange about this. Very strange. A phone call from three miles away, five minutes after leaving the house? Now, he could have made the call from there, because that is where they had another car. They leave the van, which we must now assume was stolen, and get away in the other car. But the police could still be alerted to look out for two men and a child. After all, we can give them a pretty exact description. No, they couldn't be that stupid. Or that careless. So, why? Why?

HELENA. I think the brandy has gone to my head.

EVIE. Well I'm glad something has. The money!

HELENA. What?

EVIE. The money! Left in the greenhouse? Right at the scene of the abduction? Don't you see? It means surely that they must have a hide-out close by. In the neighbourhood. Within a radius of five miles, say. Hence the phone call from Natalie's Lane or wherever. Though I still think that was a very stupid mistake. They could have covered their tracks by waiting an hour or so before actually making the call. Even longer. The longer the better.

HELENA. No.

EVIE. What do you mean, no?

HELENA. Well ... what if they had waited too long? There was the danger we might have discovered David missing and called the police before we really knew what was happening.

EVIE. Yes. Yes, I think you may be right. So, where could they have gone to ground? Two men and a boisterous six-year-old don't easily melt into a community where virtually everybody knows everybody, at least by sight. The greenhouse ... The greenhouse ... Why, in God's name, in the greenhouse? Helena!

HELENA. What?

EVIE. Where would a kidnapper want the ransom left? Where it can be clearly seen, right? Or at least, where the surroundings can be clearly seen, in case there's a trap. The kidnapper needs a place from where he can watch while he himself is unobserved, to see if his instructions are carried out. Now, from where can the greenhouse be clearly seen? Come on! Think, woman, think! *(HELENA shakes her head.)* The kitchen garden is surrounded by a high wall. You can't see into it from anywhere but ...? *(EVIE waits expectantly but HELENA just sits staring at her.)* You can't see into it from anywhere but this house. And where, in this house, gives you the best view of the kitchen garden and whole surrounding area? The attic, you fool, the attic! Don't you understand? They're still here. They've never left. They're in the attic, kidnappers and kidnapped, because this is the last place anyone would think of looking for them. *(HELENA can do no more than sit and shake her head bemusedly.)* And, if they are in the attic, there are a lot of questions to be answered. Because it means they must have an accomplice in this house.

(JOHN appears at the double doors.)

JOHN. Madam ... luncheon is served.

CURTAIN

ACT II

AT RISE: Twelve hours later. A reading LAMP in the conservatory is switched on and, by its light, comfortable in an easy chair, EVIE is reading a book. The house beyond, and all around, is in darkness. The stove is now ALIGHT, casting a warm red glow from its face.

Through the gloom, HELENA can be seen coming down the stairs. She walks across to the double doors where she stops. She is in nightdress, dressing gown and mules. EVIE looks up at her over the top of her spectacles.

EVIE. What are you doing down here?

EVIE. I couldn't sleep.

EVIE. Take a pill.

HELENA. No! I couldn't. I couldn't possibly go to sleep, knowing those ... those men are in the house.

EVIE. You don't know that they are in the house.

HELENA. You said they were!

EVIE. Did I? *(She shakes her head.)* It was only a deduction and I could be completely wrong. They could be hundred of miles away by now.

HELENA. Do you think so?

EVIE. No. I think they're up in the attic.

HELENA. *(sliding into a seat at the table)* Yes, you're right. They are in the house. I can feel it.

EVIE. Nonsense. All you can feel are your own nerves.

HELENA. Why are you down here? Couldn't you sleep either?

EVIE. I never sleep much. I quite often come down here late at night and read. You wouldn't know about that, of course, because usually, I presume, you sleep like a log. *(She goes back to her book.)*

HELENA. *(looking around)* It's so quiet, so still.

EVIE. The countryside only gives an impression of stillness. There is plenty of activity going on all around, believe me.

HELENA. If only I knew what was going on upstairs.

EVIE. If anything.

HELENA. That poor child.

EVIE. Poor child nothing. He's either having the adventure of his life or, more than likely, he's fast asleep which is what you should be so why don't you go to bed? *(HELENA gets up to take a nervous walk around the table.)* If you're worried about the men, and what they might possibly do, take two pills. That way you won't be any the wiser.

HELENA. You can't possibly be so flippant about it.

EVIE. My flippancy, as you put it, is probably, in the long run, a lot more practical, and certainly a lot more dignified, than your hysterics. I can at least think with some semblance of logic.

HELENA. Have you decided what you're going to do?

EVIE. Sit it out.

HELENA. What?

EVIE. Well, logically speaking, I can't do anything else in the middle of the night can I?

HELENA. Yes you can. You can telephone the police. Which is what you should have done hours ago anyway.

EVIE. Really. You know, Helena, when I employed you as my companion, I honestly thought I was employing an intelligent woman. Just suppose my old china is what he says he is, a telephone engineer, or ex-telephone engineer. And, just suppose, my assumptions are correct and he is, at this moment, sitting up there in our attic. Do you think this hasn't been a carefully prepared plan? And do you think those careful preparations wouldn't include an extension to the telephone system? Any call, in or out of here, would be tapped from the attic. If you wish to be murdered in your bed, then go and telephone the police. Go on.

HELENA. We could go to them.

EVIE. And I suppose a car driving out of here at half past one in the morning wouldn't arouse suspicion? I'd hardly be going to visit the bank manager would I? And that is the only trip I'm expected to take in the next thirty-six hours.

HELENA. Well, tomorrow then.

EVIE. We'll see. Tomorrow is another day, sufficient unto it is the evil thereof.

HELENA. No! No, no, no! You've got to do something. You can't just sit there and ... and...

EVIE. And? There you are, you see. You're hardly brimming over with brilliant ideas are you?

HELENA. It's inhuman. To take it all so calmly.

EVIE. Do not let appearances deceive you. One of the basic laws of survival, young lady, is that appearances are deceptive. Nothing is what it seems. Our telephone engineers seemed to be telephone engineers and we were fooled. You know neither what I am thinking or feeling so don't pass judgement.

HELENA. I'm sorry. *(pause)* I know you must be suffering...

EVIE. And don't get mawkish. That's the last thing I need. Now, may I return to my book? I was just at a very exciting part.

HELENA. I think you must have a plan.

EVIE. *(Puts down her book with a heavy sigh.)* I told you, we are going to sit it out.

HELENA. But I can't see what that will do.

EVIE. The longer they have to sweat it out up there, not knowing what I will do, the jumpier they'll get. And jumpy people get careless, they make mistakes. Look what happened when the buffalo waited.

HELENA. With all due respect, two defenseless women in a lonely house miles from anywhere can hardly be equated with a buffalo. If you ask me, the buffalo are in the attic.

EVIE. Ah, then we shall just have to use our superior intellect, won't we? That is, I will have to use mine, some considerable doubt having been cast upon yours. Anyway, what makes you think we're so defenseless? There is a cupboard full of guns next door.

HELENA. I've never used a gun in my life. I wouldn't know how to.

EVIE. But I do know how to. I have medals for

marksmanship. My hand might not be as steady as it was but you don't need to be a marksman to blast off with a twelve bore.

HELENA. They might have armed themselves.

EVIE. I have the only key to the cupboard. And it has not been broken into. I checked. If they are armed, they brought the weapons in with them. Perhaps you'd feel safer if I sat here with a shotgun across my knees.

HELENA. I'd feel a lot worse.

EVIE. That's the first sensible thing you've said. Anyway, there is another reason for playing a waiting game. I intend to find out who their accomplice is.

HELENA. And how do you intend to do that?

EVIE. What do you do when there are rats in the house? You lay traps.

HELENA. What traps?

EVIE. Oh, for God's sake, Helena! Use what little noddle you've got. Rat traps are baited and, in this case, the bait is the money in the greenhouse. Then we wait for the trap to spring. Who is the real villain of the piece? That is the question. The accomplice can be one of only three people.

HELENA. Three?

EVIE. Three. John, Peters, and yourself.

HELENA. Me?

EVIE. Don't squeak, please, Helena. It's very irritating.

HELENA. Why me?

EVIE. Why not you?

HELENA. But it's ... it's ... absurd!

EVIE. Is it?

HELENA. *(showing some spirit)* Of course it is. And you know perfectly well it is.

EVIE. I know nothing of the kind. In fact, if this were an Agatha Christie plot, you would be the likeliest culprit, as being the unlikeliest suspect.

HELENA. But what possible motive could I have?

EVIE. The same as everybody else — fifty thousand motives to be exact.

HELENA. If I thought for a moment you were being serious...

EVIE. Yes?

HELENA. *(shaking her head)* I don't believe it. It's nonsense. Ridiculous.

EVIE. Remember what I said about appearances. I must admit though, the most likely person, in my view, would be Peters. The greenhouse is part of his preserve. He could keep watch from some safe hiding place. He could, while raking the lawn for example, take a signal from an attic window without arousing any suspicion. I must admit Mr. Peters comes first on my list. But that doesn't eliminate you, so don't think that it does. Now why don't you go back to bed? Lock your door and put a chair against it if you feel unsafe. Though God knows why you should. They're hardly likely to do anything silly at this stage, and molesting you would be about the silliest thing I could think of at the moment, if that is what you're worried about. *(HELENA doesn't move.)* All right then, go and make a nice cup of tea. I could do with one. Well, go on. They won't be moving about. They will have been warned about the dogs. No one wants to bump into a couple of Doberman Pinchers in the middle of the night. Do you know something, Miss Keeley? I think we hold all the cards at the moment. I think their clever plan will come unstuck. They thought, an old lady? She'll go to pieces. She'll be ... what's the expression? ... a pushover. Well, I don't think they are going to find it that easy.

HELENA. I don't think we hold all the cards. They have the ace of trumps. They have David.

EVIE. We'll see about that. Now how about that tea?

(HELENA nods, gets up from the table and goes. As she reaches the double doors, JOHN steps out from behind them. HELENA shrieks and falls back into the conservatory still screaming hysterically. JOHN tries to quiet her. EVIE, who started and dropped her book with the first shriek, gets out of her chair. Helena is standing with her back against the table, still screaming, as EVIE walks up to her. JOHN is fluttering, burbling apologies, mainly to EVIE.)

JOHN. I'm sorry. I'm sorry. I didn't mean to frighten her. I didn't do anything.

EVIE. Helena! Miss Keeley! Stop that. Stop it this instant. *(But HELENA is obviously not going to stop and EVIE slaps her hard across the face. HELENA shuts up and sits down with a thump.)*

JOHN. I'm sorry. I really am sorry. But what did she do that for?

EVIE. It was enough to give anybody a fright, suddenly appearing like that, out of the dark.

HELENA. He's always doing it. He does it deliberately.

Creeps around the place. He does it to frighten me.

Evie. Well, there's no doubt he succeeded, but I don't think he did it intentionally.

John. Of course not. What would I want to do that for?

Helena. I don't know why you do it! You're perverted!

Evie. That's enough! Anyway, why are you still roaming around at this time of night? And what were you doing skulking behind there?

John. I heard voices so I came down to see what was happening.

Evie. You could have come half way down the stairs, seen it was us in here, and gone back up again.

John. I came down the back stairs.

Evie. How long have you been here?

John. I got to the door just as she did.

Evie. I don't believe you. You've been standing there listening to our conversation.

John. I tell you I just got there.

Evie. All right, all right. Well, now that you're here, kindly help this panicky lady into the kitchen and make a pot of tea.

Helena. I don't need any help, thank you. Certainly not from him.

Evie. I don't care whether you do or not. Just go.

(HELENA gets to her feet and goes, followed by JOHN. EVIE watches them go then returns to her chair to pick up her book. She goes over to a cupboard and puts the book away, locking the cupboard with a key she carries on a chatelaine, then she follows the

others out. The LIGHTS DIM. There is the sound of CHILD NOISES. Then the LIGHTS slowly come up — first red, and then into the whiteness of day. As they do so, the CHILD NOISES fade and pop sound of the RADIO comes up. JOHN Enters from around the corner of the conservatory. He is wearing his butcher's apron again. He goes over to the tall cupboard and opens it. It has no shelves and contains only a couple of brooms, mops, cleaning things. There are three or four large coathooks of the old Victorian type. JOHN takes a broom and closes the cupboard doors. As he does so, there is the sound of a CAR pulling up outside. He crosses over to look out into the garden, then moves quickly to disappear around the corner. A moment later EVIE Enters from the garden. She is wearing hat and coat and carries an old carpet bag which she places on the table. She takes off her hat and puts that on the table too. JOHN reappears, keeping himself concealed as much as possible behind the corner and the tree. Presumably unaware that JOHN is watching her, EVIE takes a wad of notes from the carpet bag, holds them in one hand and flaps the wad against the palm of her other hand as she ruminates. Then she puts the notes back into the bag. She picks up her hat and crosses to the cupboard, opens it, hangs up her hat, takes off her coat, hangs that up too. Then she returns to the table. She looks around as though to make sure she is unobserved. JOHN retreats a little into the corner. Then EVIE picks up the bag and goes out into the garden. JOHN comes out of concealment and crosses back to where he can watch EVIE'S progress across the garden. HELENA appears from the house, sees JOHN, disappears for a second to switch off the radio, and reappears. JOHN turns to regard her then looks out across the garden again.)

JOHN. She's got the money.

HELENA. What are you talking about?

JOHN. The old girl. She's been to the bank and got the money.

HELENA. So you were listening last night.

JOHN. What if I was?

HELENA. You heard everything?

JOHN. I heard a thing or two. Put that with the way you two were carrying on yesterday, like a couple of cats on hot bricks, it doesn't take much to put two and two together.

HELENA. What do you know?

JOHN. I got it all worked out.

HELENA. Maybe you had it all worked out right from the beginning. What are you going to do now? Wait until it's dark and collect the money? *(JOHN turns away from the window and slowly advances on HELENA who backs away.)*

JOHN. You know something? You talk too much. Your mouth is too big for your own good.

HELENA. What are you doing? Stay away from me! *(JOHN stops and leans on his broom.)*

JOHN. Are you really frightened of me? *(HELENA nods. JOHN shaking his head.)* But why? I've never done anything to make you frightened. Not on purpose. Do you hate me?

HELENA. No, of course not. Why should I hate you?

JOHN. *(regarding HELENA intently)* I'm not very good-looking. *(pause)* But that's not my fault. Is it?

HELENA. *(a self-conscious laugh)* Well, we can't all be ... I'm not exactly ... well ... too pretty ... or anything.

JOHN. You have nice eyes.

HELENA. Do I? *(another self-conscious laugh)* Well, I don't know what's nice about them.

JOHN. Yes. Nice eyes. *(He leans forward on his broom.)*

HELENA. Did madam really get the money? *(JOHN nods.)* But how could she have...? *(got such a large sum immediately from a small country bank)*

JOHN. I saw her, in here. She took it out of her old carpet bag. I saw her.

HELENA. What reason could she have possibly given for withdrawing such a large sum?

JOHN. She'd think of something.

HELENA. Yes, but a small branch...

JOHN. Do you think I'm ugly? *(HELENA shakes her head.)* Well then, if you don't think I'm ugly, maybe you could get to like me. I would like us to be friends. I've never had many friends. Since you've been here you've hardly talked to me at all. It would be nice if you could like me.

HELENA. I never said I didn't like you.

JOHN. Oh, so you do like me then?

HELENA. Yes ... yes ... of course I like you.

JOHN. That's nice. You don't know anything about me but you like me. It's an instinctive liking for me, is it?

HELENA. Look, I don't know why you...?

JOHN. I just want to know where I stand, that's all. I mean, supposing you didn't know me as I am ... supposing you didn't know I worked here ... supposing I was rich ... would that make you like me more?

HELENA. But you're not rich.

JOHN. I might be one day. One day all this could be mine. *(He waves an arm around indicating the house.)*

HELENA. *(laughing)* And pigs can fly. *(JOHN stares at*

HELENA. Silence.)

JOHN. I don't like people laughing at me.

HELENA. I'm sorry. It's just that ... the whole notion is so absurd.

JOHN. Why?

HELENA. Because ... Oh, this is riduculous!

JOHN. WHY?

HELENA. Don't shout at me please. There is no need to lose your self-control.

JOHN. You don't even know the way you talk to me, do you? You don't know how it hurts, to be treated like dirt.

HELENA. I don't mean to. I'm sorry. I didn't realize ... *(suddenly)* ... Are you thinking of fifty thousand pounds as being rich? *(JOHN turns away and looks out of the window.)* So it is you.

JOHN. What is me?

HELENA. The accomplice.

JOHN. What are you talking about?

HELENA. Anyway, it isn't even fifty thousand, not split three ways.

JOHN. I wasn't talking about that.

HELENA. Then what were you talking about?

JOHN. I would have told you, but you wouldn't listen.

HELENA. All right, I'm listening now.

JOHN. *(shaking his head)* I don't think you'd ever listen to someone like me. You would just laugh. *(He lays his broom against the window sill, turns and advances on HELENA.)*

HELENA. Anyway, I don't kow why we're talking about ... all this kind of thing ... at a time like this ... when ... what are you doing?

JOHN. *(holding out his hand)* I found your secateurs. Don't you want them?

HELENA. Oh. Thank you.

JOHN. Here you are then.

HELENA. Where did you find them?

JOHN. Out there ... where you left them. Here you are. *(HELENA stands deadstill, looking at JOHN holding out the secateurs, then she slowly advances and, when just within reach, stretches out her hand. As her hand opens to take the secateurs, JOHN makes a short, swift, stabbing motion. HELENA gasps and hurriedly withdraws the hand. JOHN advances. HELENA retreats. Then she turns, as though to run through the doors and into the house, but JOHN is suddenly between her and the door, still threatening with the secateurs. Again HELENA backs away, again JOHN advances, the cat playing with the mouse. This time HELENA turns for the garden door but, once more, she finds JOHN has got between her and freedom. She retreats. He advances. Now she tries for the far end of the conservatory but JOHN is too quick for her. HELENA is, by now, almost in a state of collapse. She starts to whimper. JOHN lunges. HELENA almost falls over the table and then, finding it between her and her assailant, she uses it as a barrier. He stabs to the left, to the right, feints, more than attempts to hit, and she evades his moves.)*

HELENA. Don't ... please ... don't ... *(He stabs again.)* Why are you doing this? ... Why? *(She suddenly sees she is closer to the house doors than he is and makes a dash for them. But JOHN grabs her by one arm and swings her back. He puts both arms around her and starts kissing her passionately. Then, with one arm holding her, secateurs in that hand, he tries with the other hand to get at the buttons of her blouse or to rip it. HELENA struggles.)* No! No! *(Now, in a fury, JOHN grabs her by the arm and withdrawing the other, threatens her with the secateurs, moving them in front of her face.*

JOHN. Don't say no! Don't say it!

EVIE. JOHN!

(EVIE has Entered the conservatory from the garden. JOHN lets go of HELENA and turns to face EVIE. HELENA almost collapses, falls against a bench and starts to sob. JOHN and EVIE stand and glare at each other.)

EVIE. Get out of here. *(JOHN opens his mouth to say something.)* Get out! *(JOHN moves slowly towards the bench. He is grinning and, as he approaches, HELENA cringes. JOHN gently places the secateurs on the bench next to HELENA and turns away to walk past EVIE towards the garden door.)* I'll deal with you later. *(She turns to HELENA.)* Helena ... *(But HELENA runs from the room and totters up the stairs. EVIE turns back to JOHN now standing by the garden door.)* Well? *(JOHN shrugs. He is still grinning, like a naughty schoolboy found out in some small misdemeanor.)* You do realize how serious this is?

JOHN. I wasn't going to hurt her.

EVIE. You attacked her. You attempted to rape her. God knows what would have happened if I hadn't ... You weren't going to hurt her! *(EVIE slowly shakes her head, for once at a loss.)* That frozen piece of English cod couldn't possibly have given you the come-on. Are you out of your mind? Well ... the harm has been done now, not as bad as it might have been, but dangerous nevertheless. The question now is, what am I going to do about it? What is she going to do about it? One thing's for certain — she's not going to forget it.

JOHN. *(an attempt to mitigate his own behavior)* Ask her why she attacked me.

HELENA. What?

JOHN. *(waggling a finger towards the bench)* Yes. She did. Yesterday morning. She attacked me with a knife.

EVIE. What is going on in this house? Has everyone gone mad? What do you mean, she attacked you? What were you doing?

JOHN. Nothing. I came in here ... she was standing there ... doing something with flowers ... Before I knew what happened, she turned round and cut me with the pruning knife. She said it was because I gave her a fright.

EVIE. How did you give her a fright?

JOHN. I didn't give her a fright.

EVIE. You must have done something.

JOHN. I tell you I didn't do anything!

EVIE. No? Like a minute ago? I suppose you weren't doing anything then. We imagined it, did we?

JOHN. I don't know what came over me.

EVIE. We both know what came over you. And I also know what the result could be. For forty years I have lived in this house, for forty years the respected wife of a respected English gentleman. No one has been able to open any cupboards or rattle any skeletons. No one has entertained the slightest suspicion that all was not as it appeared to be. And now, suddenly, in one day, everything is threatened. First by a bunch of criminal lunatics and now you.

JOHN. She won't do anything. I'll tell her I'm sorry. I'll plead with her, beg her not to do anything.

EVIE. Yes. You certainly WILL apologize. And then you'll leave everything else to me. If you weren't a fact of my life I've managed to keep the world in ignorance of...

JOHN. Only to protect yourself. What is it to me who knows? What does it matter?

EVIE. If, when I die — which, if I can help it, won't be for a good few years yet — you want all this ... *(indicating the house)* ... to be yours, then it had better matter to you. God only knows what would have happened to you if the Colonel hadn't been idiot enough to accept you.

JOHN. He accepted anything from you.

EVIE. So just remember what I have done for you.

JOHN. *(sneering)* Of course. But how can I be sure? How do I know that all this is going to be mine?

EVIE. You don't. But another indiscretion like that ... *(pointing to where the indiscretion took place)* ... and you will know for certain that it isn't.

JOHN. And why are you trying to keep me in the dark about the other thing that's going on?

EVIE. What other thing?

JOHN. Look ... there's nobody around ... What's going on?

EVIE. Are you sure you don't already know?

JOHN. If I knew, I wouldn't be asking.

EVIE. David has been kidnapped. *(JOHN nods.)* The kidnappers have demanded fifty thousand pounds. *(JOHN nods.)* To be left in the greenhouse. Which is where I have left it.

JOHN. Who did it?

EVIE. A pair of bogus telephone engineers.

JOHN. *(still nodding)* Where do you suppose they've taken him? The kid?

EVIE. How would I know?

JOHN. You're just going to let them have the money?

EVIE. What else would you suggest?

JOHN. Why haven't you been to the police? Afraid?

EVIE. You're a fool. It's not merely the police. What do you suppose would happen if this leaked out? As it certainly would. The son of a well-known businessman kidnapped! It would be front page news, not only here but all over the world. And all of us would be a part of that news. This place would be swarming with newsmen, television people. We'd be harassed to death. One good news story could easily lead to another. Do you understand what I am saying? *(JOHN nods.)* So, for the moment, it is a situation that I can, and will, handle on my own.

(HELENA is seen, coming down the stairs. As EVIE has her back to the house, it is JOHN who sees her and silently indicates to EVIE that she is coming. EVIE turns to see her. HELENA is carrying a coat and a small suitcase. EVIE shoos JOHN away with her hand and, taking his broom, he goes out through the garden door. EVIE gets a sewing basket and some sewing work from a cupboard and crosses over to her favorite chair which she moves so that she can look directly out across the garden. HELENA, having reached the bottom of the stairs, places her suitcase and coat behind the door, just out of sight.)

EVIE. Ah, Helena ... Are you all right?

HELENA. *(Shakes her head.)* I'm leaving. I'd like to call a cab to drive me into the village.

EVIE. Leaving? But why?

HELENA. I couldn't stay in this house another moment.

EVIE. You're being melodramatic.

HELENA. *(She opens and closes her mouth two or three times before she finally finds words.)* I'm being what? After what happened?

EVIE. You weren't hurt.

HELENA. By the grace of God I wasn't hurt.

EVIE. By the intervention of Evie you weren't hurt.

HELENA. And what if you hadn't arrived? At that moment?

EVIE. But I did arive at that moment ... So there is no reason for you to leave. He is certainly not going to try anything like that again, is he?

HELENA. How can you say that?

EVIE. I give you my personal assurance that, as far as JOHN is concerned, you have nothing to fear. He lost his head and nearly caused a tragedy. I admit that. There are times when we all lose our heads and behave foolishly. But the tragedy was averted and, as long as you are feeling all right, that is what matters most. He is full of remorse and wants to apologize.

HELENA. And that ... that ... You make it sound as if it were nothing more than ... than ... as if he'd done nothing worse than spill a cup of tea. You think an apology is all that is needed?

EVIE. He is most contrite.

HELENA. I don't believe it. Now may I please call a cab?

EVIE. No, I'm afraid not.

HELENA. Why not?

EVIE. Because you are not going anywhere.

HELENA. Mrs. Webster, my mind is made up. I am leaving this house this very minute. I can come back for the rest of my things when all this is over.

EVIE. Ah, so you haven't forgotten then? About David.

HELENA. How could I?

EVIE. I thought you must have, otherwise you wouldn't want to leave especially since there is really no reason why you should.

HELENA. There is every reason. I have never been so afraid in my life. If you won't let me call, I will walk up the road and hitch a lift.

EVIE. Walk out on me? Just like that? Walk out on David?

HELENA. I told you what to do about David. You should have called the police hours ago. You should have called his parents!

EVIE. Why?

HELENA. Because they should know what is going on.

EVIE. They would be upset for nothing. The money is in the greenhouse. The kidnappers will collect it and leave. There is no need for them to harm the child as the child has not left this house. The situation, if nobody behaves foolishly by losing their head, will soon be back to normal. So why don't you sit down and keep me company for a while? (*But HELENA doesn't sit down. She stands staring at EVIE who calmly goes on with her sewing. After a moment*

EVIE looks up.) Miss Keeley, what do you suppose would happen if you did try to leave?

HELENA. You wouldn't think of stopping me by force.

EVIE. No, not I. But, if you were to be seen leaving this house, it will be thought by watching eyes that you are going for help and you will not get very far.

HELENA. You mean...

EVIE. That's exactly what I mean. I don't suppose they would kill you. On the other hand I can't see them being too gentle with you either. There is always the risk as well, if you did manage to get away, that they might not be too gentle with David. I am surprised you did not think of it. Apart from a certain loyalty I expect from you, towards me, I am more than a little surprised that you would be prepared to leave a child in the lurch, a child for whom you have always expressed a touching devotion. Now, are you going to sit down and keep me company? Or, better still, what has happened to the running of this house? Life must go on, you know, and the going on of life includes my morning coffee which I haven't had yet.

HELENA. Is it only a day since those men appeared? It seems like ... a hundred years.

EVIE. Tomorrow it will all be over. Helena, I want to ask a favor of you. In fact, I want to ask you to promise me something.

HELENA. Yes?

EVIE. When it is all over, when the men have left with their loot and David has been restored to us, I want you to say nothing about what has happened.

HELENA. I don't understand. Surely the police will have to be told.

EVIE. No. I am the only one who will have suffered a loss and that, quite simply, only in financial terms and I do not want that loss to be compounded by the loss of my privacy. I do not want my life made a misery by all the publicity — newspapers, television. I am an old woman, a solitary person in a way. I want to spend my time in peace and quiet which is one of the reasons why I have continued to live in this huge, old house. I do not want the great unwashed public trampling all over my flower-beds, peering in through windows, blocking the drive with their motor cars.

HELENA. You could charge them a sightseeing fee and recoup your losses.

EVIE. I am not joking, Helena.

HELENA. I'm sorry. But I don't see how you can keep it quiet. There's Roland and Penny to begin with. They'll have to know. David will tell them even if no one else does.

EVIE. Roland and Penny are family. They will respect my wishes. I hope you will too. Also, I should think, they would want to keep it quiet to avoid the chance of any repetition. The child could become a target for any monster who decides to be a copycat. No, all in all, it would be much better if nothing was said. Do you agree? *(HELENA does not answer. EVIE smiling.)* You can put it in your memoirs one day. *(pause)* I hope you will be with me a long time, Helena. And I will certainly see to it that loyal service is rewarded. Now, how about that coffee? *(HELENA nods and starts to go.)* And, if you see John, find out what delicious surprise he's got for lunch.

*(HELENA goes. The LIGHTS change and once more, the CHILD
NOISES are heard. It is night. The only light is from the MOON,
and the red GLOW of the stove. EVIE is still in her chair and has
fallen asleep. A FIGURE appears at the garden door, stops for a
moment, and then opens the door. It is JOHN. He stands looking
at EVIE and then, closing the door behind him, he advances
silently towards her. He stands in front of her chair and then
crouches beside her and touches her arm, gives it a little
shake.)*

JOHN. Wake up.

EVIE. What! ... Oh, John ... What are you doing?

JOHN. I've got something to tell you. Something's
happened. *(pause)* Peters is dead.

EVIE. What?

JOHN. *(nodding)* I've just found him, in the pond by
the summerhouse.

EVIE. Are you sure?

JOHN. What, that he's dead? *(He giggles.)* You don't find
a body floating in a pond and not be sure. I should think
he's got enough mud inside him to sink a battleship.

EVIE. How did he die?

JOHN. You mean you don't think he drowned?

EVIE. You don't drown easily in a few inches of
water.

JOHN. You do if you trip up first and hit your head
before you hit the water.

EVIE. There are marks? On his head? Where?

JOHN. Look, however he died, take it from me he's as

dead as a doornail. I've put him in the summerhouse.

EVIE. What did you do that for?

JOHN. Later, I'll take him down to the river and throw him in. It's easier to drown in a river than a pond. He could have stumbled on the bank, tripped over a root or something. No questions will be asked.

EVIE. He didn't drown, did he? I mean, not by accident.

JOHN. Look, I don't know what happened to him. But you said you didn't want any questions asked, that's why I thought of the river. I'm doing it for you, just to make sure nobody asks any questions. I thought I was being clever.

EVIE. Yes. Yes. What were you doing out there?

JOHN. I went out to let the dogs loose.

EVIE. Did you see anybody else out there?

JOHN. No.

EVIE. The money! *(She gets to her feet and goes to the window to look out.)*

JOHN. It's gone. I looked in the greenhouse. There's nothing there.

EVIE. Maybe Peters took it. Maybe he was carrying it and dropped it somewhere.

JOHN. No. I looked. It's gone.

EVIE. What were you looking for? *(She switches on her reading light.)*

JOHN. Your old bag. Your old carpet bag.

EVIE. How did YOU know the money was in there?

JOHN. Well I ... I ... saw you with it, didn't I? I saw you going into the kitchen garden with it. And, when you came back, you didn't have it.

EVIE. It's my fault. I fell asleep. I sat here so I could keep watch on the garden and I fell asleep. Where could it have gone to? Where? Unless ... unless one of them came down and took it.

JOHN. Yes.

EVIE. *(Turns to look at him.)* Unless one of who came down from where?

JOHN. One of the men from the ... *(silence)*

EVIE. So you did know. You knew all along.

JOHN. Helena told me!

EVIE. You lie.

JOHN. Well I just knew then. I put two and two together. Like I said to her, it doesn't take much to do that. *(silence)* Well why are you looking at me like that? If you're fifty thousand pounds poorer, I'm fifty thousand pounds poorer, aren't I?

EVIE. Are you waiting for me to die?

JOHN. No! But it's true, isn't it? I got to protect what's mine, haven't I?

EVIE. Alright. Supposing one of them did come down and collect the money, he could have killed Peters for his share. But, if that is what happened, surely they would have left?

JOHN. Maybe I should go up and take a look.

EVIE. No.

JOHN. I could take the dogs.

EVIE. No. There's the child. *(She sinks into her chair.)* Someone in this house is playing a very funny game.

JOHN. I tell you what, I'll go and take another look in the garden. I'll really look carefully this time. Everywhere. Maybe it was dropped somewhere and I missed it.

Or maybe Peters hid it. Yes! That's it. He hid it somewhere.

EVIE. You mean, he really did die by accident?

JOHN. He could have. I don't know, do I?

EVIE. Somehow I very much doubt it.

JOHN. I'll go and look anyway.

(EVIE nods. JOHN goes out into the garden. EVIE sits in her chair, thinking. HELENA appears at the door to the house.)

HELENA. I'm going up now. Is there anything you want before I go?

EVIE. No thank you. *(She turns to look at her.)* Where have you been?

HELENA. Sitting in the kitchen, reading.

EVIE. Romantic novels again? *(HELENA admits it with a smile.)* The Colonel used to like thrillers. Nothing like a good thriller, he used to say, to get your mind off things.

HELENA. You must be tired.

EVIE. No.

HELENA. Why don't you go to bed? *(pause)* It's not going to do any good sitting there. *(pause)* You're watching, aren't you? *(pause)* Has anything happened?

EVIE. Nothing has happened.

HELENA. I'll go up then.

EVIE. Yes.

HELENA. Good night.

EVIE. Good night. *(HELENA starts to go.)* Oh, there is something you can do before you go. If you'd just pass me my book? *(pointing)* It's in the cupboard there, top shelf.

HELENA. It wouldn't be a romantic novel, I suppose. *(She opens the cupboard, takes out the book, closes the cupboard.)*

EVIE. No. It's political philosophy.

HELENA. I didn't know you were interested in politics.

EVIE. There you are you see ... more surprises. *(HELENA glance idly at the book as she starts back towards EVIE.)*

HELENA. Nietzsche. It's in German.

EVIE. Of course. I do speak the language. And I believe that authors should always be read in the original, if possible. Do you speak any language? Other than English?

HELENA. Schoolgirl French.

EVIE. Which wouldn't get you very far in France.

HELENA. I suppose not. This book's got a swastika in it. It's been stamped with an eagle and a swastika, and some printing. Can't read it. Looks as if it's been rubbed away.

EVIE. It's a souvenir from the war.

HELENA. Oh, how interesting.

EVIE. The Colonel brought quite a lot of stuff back from Germany after the war. May I? *(She holds out her hand for the book.)*

HELENA. Oh. Sorry. *(She hands the book over.)* Well, I'll leave you to your book then. And your politics.

EVIE. Yes. Goodnight.

HELENA. Goodnight. *(But HELENA doesn't move. She stands there, obviously wanting to say something else. After a moment or two EVIE looks up from her book.)* I wanted to say ...

I think ... that is ... well, I'm trying very hard ... I'm trying very hard, not to panic ... for him ... David, I mean ... and for you ... You are a remarkable woman ... I don't know how you can be so ... so calm ... so brave. I'm trying to be like that ... but it's not easy. I keep wanting ... feeling like crying like ... trembling and ... and ... I don't know if I can go on without breaking. I have this terrible feeling in my stomach ... all the time. Are you sure they're here? Are you sure they've been here all the time? Maybe that's what they wanted us to think. Maybe we've been led up the garden path to ... think that. Maybe they're not in the house at all! Oh, please dear God, say they're not in the house!

EVIE. Helena, I don't know. I don't know what is happening any more than you do. But I have obeyed the instructions. We can only wait and see. *(very gently)* Come along now, pull yourself together. You'll be all right. All right. *(HELENA nods. She is obviously very shaky.)* Why don't you go to bed now? Hmm? I tell you what, go to the kitchen and make yourself a nice hot toddy — a stiff one. And take it up to bed with you. Go on. Use rum, or whiskey and plenty of sugar.

HELENA. I'm not used to spirits.

EVIE. All the better. *(HELENA turns and goes.)*

(The LIGHTS change. The CHILD-NOISES are heard — louder now, more intense. EVIE is reading and, when the LIGHTS change back, BILL appears from around the corner of the conservatory. He is wearing a rough pair of slacks, open neck shirt and, with his index finger crooked through the tag, he is holding a jacket slung over his shoulder. He stands, for a moment, looking at EVIE.)

BILL. Hello, me old china. *(EVIE lowers her book and looks up. She is not in the least surprised. BILL moves in towards her.)* How are you then?

EVIE. As well as can be expected — in the circumstances.

BILL. Yeh. It's a bit hard on you, I suppose. Still, you're a game old bird, aren't you? Where's the other one?

EVIE. I believe she's in her bedroom.

BILL. Taking it badly is she?

EVIE. What would you expect?

BILL. She'll get over it.

EVIE. Oh, of course. *(BILL looks at her sharply.)* She will be completely unmarked by her little ordeal. Is that why you left your den? To find out how we were?

BILL. *(Shrugs.)* No. Thought I'd just take a mosey around.

EVIE. How's the child?

BILL. Little Dave? Oh, he's fine ... fine. He's a real lad, isn't he? No, you got no worry on that score, missus. Fast asleep, as a matter of fact. Which is hardly surprising, after what he put away. I mean, I know kids have appetites, but his! It's bloody ridiculous. I have never seen so many tins of baked beans disappear so fast down one gullet. I tell you, tomorrow morning he'll be farting fit to bust. He'll blow away like a balloon that's lost its string.

EVIE. He's enjoying himself then.

BILL. What? Having the time of his life.

EVIE. Yes.

BILL. *(Throws himself into a chair, stretching out his legs and lounging back.)* Of course he has asked for his Mummy once or twice. you know. But, well, we told him how she's on holiday an' that and having a lovely time, and how she'll bring him back lots of presents, so that's alright. You'd be surprised what we've promised him: a bicycle, a yacht, a pony. Anything his little heart desires. I tell you, he thinks it's all his birthdays rolled into one.

EVIE. And where is your lightfingered friend?

BILL. Oh, he's up there with him. Sleeping as well as a matter of fact. I couldn't get off. It's a bit parky up there once the sun goes down and my old bones were complaining a bit. Nice and warm down here though. Ah, what it is to be young, hey? Me old darling?

EVIE. What, indeed?

BILL. I bet you were a bit of a ... hot stuff in your time, hey? I bet you could tell a story or two. *(He winks and clicks his teeth.)*

EVIE. I think I could have handled you without too much trouble.

BILL. That wouldn't surprise me. What? Eat half a dozen like me for breakfast, hey? *(He laughs.)* Yeh, funny old world in'it?

EVIE. In what way?

BILL. Oh, nothing in particular. Just thinking of the way it goes.

EVIE. Tell me, Mr. telephone engineer, do you have any children?

BILL. Now ... I didn't come down here to talk about me, did I?

EVIE. What did you come down for?

BILL. I told you, take a shufty round, see what's

happening like.

EVIE. And what would you expect to be happening?

BILL. Well ... you got the money then. *(EVIE nods.)* Yeh. I saw you take it into the greenhouse. At least I saw you take something into the greenhouse. The only trouble is, I haven't see it come out of the greenhouse.

EVIE. Really? You mean your accomplice has failed to deliver?

BILL. Accomplice ... *(He chuckles.)* ... There's a nice old-fashioned word for you.

EVIE. When was he supposed to make the pick-up?

BILL. Now ... *(He chuckles again and wags a naughty-naughty finger at her.)* ... you don't really expect me to give away trade secrets do you? "When" means "Who." *(He has crossed over to the bench, which he now sits on, not noticing the pinholder. He leaps up.)* Ow! *(looking around and picking up the pinholder)* What's that?

EVIE. It's a pinholder. For arranging flowers.

BILL. *(crossing back upstage)* A guy could get hurt around here if he ain't careful. *(He puts down the pinholder.)*

EVIE. How true. For example, your accomplice is dead.

BILL. I don't believe you.

EVIE. Believe what you like, And the money has disappeared.

BILL. What are you up to?

EVIE. I am not up to anything. Isn't there an old saying about when thieves fall out? What is that old saying?

BILL. The money has gone? I mean, gone?

EVIE. It would appear so.

BILL. Now watch it, missus. Just watch it. We've still

got the kid, remember.

EVIE. I am well aware of that fact. *(BILL frowns again in heavy concentration, thinking hard.)*

BILL. Gone from the greenhouse you mean. You mean, taken from the greenhouse, and gone?

EVIE. That is exactly what I mean. Permutate it as many ways as you wish, it still comes to the same thing.

BILL. *(Gets up and paces for a moment, thinking hard, trying to put together the pieces of the jigsaw. He is a very confused man. He stops, facing EVIE.)* I don't get it.

EVIE. And, at this rate, you're not likely to, either.

BILL. Don't make jokes, lady. I'm not in the mood for funnies. I think you know more than you're letting on. Let's see ... *(He looks at the position of EVIE'S chair to the windows.)* How long you been sitting there?

EVIE. I assure you, I am as much in the dark as you appear to be. All I know is, your accomplice is dead.

BILL. How?

EVIE. How do I know? Or how did he die?

BILL. How did he die?

EVIE. Supposedly by drowning ... in a pond. If you don't believe me, take a look in the summerhouse. *(pause)*

BILL. Oh, no ... oho no ... You're clever ... *(laughing)* ... very clever. Take a look in the summerhouse. I nearly fell for that. Do you think I don't know there's two bloody great man-eating dogs out there?

EVIE. I never even thought of that. Isn't that funny?

BILL. Very funny. And I told you, I'm in no mood for funnies. Now look ... I don't want to turn nasty, that's not

my way ... But if you think you can put one over on me ...
(*He throws away his jacket and grabs EVIE by an arm.*) Come
on, out with it. Let's have the truth.

EVIE. You're hurting me!

BILL. I haven't started, lady.

(*JOHN appears in the doorway to the house and, as BILL takes
both EVIE'S arms and pulls her to her feet, he moves swiftly and
silently towards them, pausing for a fraction of a second to pick up
the pinholder.*)

BILL. Now you tell me what's going on or, so help me,
I won't ... (*JOHN brings the pin-holder down on BILL'S back.
With a scream of pain, BILL lets go of EVIE and straightens up.
For a moment it is almost like a tableau before he swings around to
face his assailant. Now, for the first time, we see his exposed back.
The pin-holder has ripped part of the shirt and the flesh beneath to
ribbons, both shirt and back and spattered with blood.*) You!

(*JOHN brings the pin-holder down again, this time straight into
BILL'S face. A short, sharp scream is smothered by BILL'S hands
as they fly to his face. He manages to barge past JOHN, shoving
him bodily out of the way, and staggers blindly towards the doors to
the house. He falls to his knees and JOHN, recovering from having
been knocked completely off balance, wields the pin-holder again.
Squealing with pain, BILL lurches towards the corner of the conservatory with JOHN in pursuit. As they disappear around the
corner there is the sound of scuffling and another SCREAM. EVIE
disappears after the two men. Another SCREAM, cut short, then
silence. HELENA appears in her night attire, coming down the
stairs. She reaches the door to the conservatory and stops, looking*

around, somewhat surprised to find the conservatory empty, particularly as EVIE'S reading lamp is still on. The book is lying on the floor and HELENA crosses over to pick it up. She places the book on EVIE'S chair and looks around again. There is a NOISE from behind the corner. HELENA hesitates for a moment and then moves towards the source of the noise. She is half way there when EVIE appears.)

EVIE. What are you doing in here?

HELENA. I heard noises, a scream.

EVIE. You've been having a nightmare.

HELENA. I wasn't asleep.

EVIE. Then you imagined it. Are you drunk?

HELENA. I think I am a little bit. You said to take a hot toddy and I did.

(EVIE stares at her coldly. JOHN appears from around the corner, sees HELENA and quickly backs away. There is blood on his shirt. He stays within earshot.)

HELENA. I thought I heard a scream, someone screaming. I'm sorry. I must have imagined it. I'll go back now. *(She sways towards the door, stops and turns.)* Roland and Penny should be here soon.

EVIE. What?

HELENA. They should be here soon.

EVIE. What are you talking about?

HELENA. I called them at the hotel. In London. I told them. They're coming straight back. They should be here soon. I meant to tell you earlier but I didn't have the courage. They'll be here soon. Good night.

(HELENA makes her unsteady way upstairs. JOHN comes out of his hiding place.)

JOHN. The stupid bitch! What are we going to do? *(EVIE doesn't move.)* Don't just stand there! What are we going to do? *(silence)* We'll have to get the other one down.

EVIE. The other one will come down in his own good time.

JOHN. There isn't any time. *(EVIE goes over to the doors to the house and picks up a piece of paper from the telephone table. She looks at it and then lifts the telephone receiver and dials a number. She waits.)*

EVIE. Yes, I would like to speak to Mr. or Mrs. Thompson. I'm afraid I don't know their room number ... I see. What time was that ... Thank you. *(EVIE puts down the phone and turns to look at JOHN.)* They left half an hour ago. There is plenty of time. If I am right, Helena's telephone call was instrumental in bringing the first one down. Oh, he wouldn't necessarily be afraid of Roland and Penny, but he might have wanted to speed things up as they obviously weren't going the way he planned. *(She glances up towards the ceiling.)* Now this one, when he's had time to think and, with the continued absence of his friend, he will come down to find out what is happening.

JOHN. Why don't we just go up and get him? I could send the dogs in.

EVIE. No. He still has the child. He'll use the child to protect himself. Let him come down. In his own time. It shouldn't take too long.

(EVIE turns and disappears in the direction of the kitchen. JOHN stands for a moment and then he too turns away and goes around the corner of the conservatory. The LIGHTS change and once again we hear the CHILD NOISES, only now they are horribly distorted. The LIGHTS change back and DELL appears at the doors to the house. He looks around carefully and then Enters the conservatory, still looking around, treading warily, very nervous. He tries to look out of the window into the darkness of the garden. He gives this up and circles the room until he is standing facing the tall cupboard. He stretches out his hand towards the key just as EVIE appears from the direction of the kitchen. She is carrying a tray covered with a cloth.)

EVIE. So you've decided to come down as well, have you? *(At the first sound of EVIE'S voice, DELL jumps a mile and, as she puts down her tray, he stands watching her warily.)* Are you hungry? *(DELL shakes his head.)* I am. I'm ravenous. *(She lifts the tray cloth and comes out with a drumstick at which she takes an appreciative bite.)* Are you sure? There's plenty there for two.

DELL. Where's Bill?

EVIE. Bill ... so that's his name. Is that his real name?

DELL. Where is he?

EVIE. I thought you were asleep. He said he left you sleeping. I take it David is still asleep. It's marvelous what children sleep through. Are you sure you wouldn't like something? *(Again, DELL shakes his head.)* You've been stuffing yourself with baked beans as well, have you?

DELL. I like baked beans.

EVIE. I'll get you some baked beans.

DELL. I don't want anything! ... Thank you. Where's Bill?

EVIE. Somewhere out there I suppose. *(She waves her drumstick towards the windows.)*

DELL. What's he doing out there?

EVIE. Why don't you go and find out?

DELL. Me? Go out there?

EVIE. Why not? You're not afraid of the dark are you?

DELL. Don't be stupid.

EVIE. Oh, I see. you're afraid that, if you do go out, I'll take the opportunity to slip upstairs. Well, I'm afraid I'm too old to go hunting around attics. In fact, I've never been up there, all the time I've lived in this house.

DELL. Where's the other lady?

EVIE. In her room. I don't think she's in any fit state to go hunting in attics either. What is it like up there?

DELL. Big.

EVIE. Well it would be. It's a big house.

DELL. It seems to go on for miles. I reckon you could almost get lost up there. And it's cold. We got in enough supplies though. We got in food, blankets.

EVIE. How long have you been planning this? *(But DELL is still too worried about the absent BILL to concentrate on EVIE.)*

BILL. Where's he got to then?

EVIE. It was a remarkably clever plan. Which one of you thought of it?

BILL. What? Oh. Well, it wasn't clever enough was it? I mean, you twigged what was goin' on. It should have been so easy. We should have been on our way out of here by now — rich!

EVIE. I don't think there can be too many get-rich-quick schemes that come off. Nice if they do, I suppose, for those concerned, but...

DELL. You don't think he's scarpered do you? Done a bunk?

EVIE. There's only one way to find out.

DELL. I can't go out there!

EVIE. Why not?

DELL. If anything goes wrong! I got to do what he tells me and he told me to stay with the kid.

EVIE. But you're not with the kid.

DELL. No. But I could scarper back there pretty quick if I had to. Out there ... anything could happen ... He'd skin me alive! *(EVIE laughs. DELL turns to look at her.)* What you laughin' at?

EVIE. You wouldn't understand. It's a private joke.

DELL. Oh, Christ! I wish he'd come back.

EVIE. Are you afraid?

DELL. If you must know, I'm shit-scared.

EVIE. But what is there to be afraid of?

DELL. *(a howl of panic)* I don't know what is happening! *(He dithers by the garden door, trying to decide whether to go out or not, then he turns back to EVIE.)* You did talk to him? I mean, he did come in here?

EVIE. Yes.

DELL. What am I going to do?

EVIE. Why don't you come here and sit down? Sit down and talk to me till he hets back. Much better that you sit down here and talk to me, have some company, than you go back up there and worry all by yourself.

Come on. We can talk about all sorts of things. We can talk about you for a start.

DELL. Talk about me? What do you want to talk about me for? There's nothing to talk about.

EVIE. I don't believe it. You're too modest. Or is it because you're shy? Bill enjoyed talking to me.

DELL. He's been away hours.

EVIE. Are you very dependent on him?

DELL. How do you mean?

EVIE. I mean, do you look up to him? Take his advice? Go along with what he says?

DELL. Most times, yeah.

EVIE. Then if you won't sit down and wait for him here, I suggest you go back upstairs, to the attic, and wait for him there.

DELL. I'll go and find him. *(He flings open the garden door and runs out. EVIE takes a cracker and a knife from the tray and starts to butter the cracker.)*

(There is a sudden baying of HOUNDS and DELL throws himself back into the room, slamming the door behind him. He is panting both with the sudden exertion and with fear.)

DELL. I forgot the bloody dogs!

EVIE. Oh, how careless of me. I didn't know they were loose. *(DELL gets off his knees, which was the position he landed in behind the door, and looks at the sleeve of his jacket.)*

DELL. Just look at that! Ripped my jacket! Those aren't dogs! They're fiends! Out of a bloody horror picture! Look at that. It could have taken my bloody arm off.

EVIE. Did it get you?

DELL. No. I was too quick for it. If I'd been quicker I could have kicked it in the bollocks at the same time. Oh, God. I think I've peed myself. No I haven't. It just felt like it. *(Still breathing hard, he flops into a chair and sits there, shaking his head. He examines his sleeve again which is pretty badly ripped.)* Phew! Boy! that was close. It's no wonder you're not scared living out here. Those things? They'd eat anybody alive given half the chance. *(suddenly)* Bill!

EVIE. Yes. that's exactly what I was thinking. Of course, that's why he hasn't come back.

DELL. You don't think they got him.

EVIE. No. We'd have heard the noise if they had got him. He probably had to make a run for it. Locked himself in a shed, or the summerhouse. I'll send John to look.

DELL. Yes ... *(Snaps his fingers.)* ... John. Send John. *(EVIE rings her handbell.)*

EVIE. Would you like a drink?

DELL. After that, yeah, I could really do with one.

EVIE. What would you like?

DELL. I don't care. Whatever you've got.

EVIE. Scotch?

DELL. Whisky? Yes.

(JOHN appears at the door. DELL glances at him before returning to examining his sleeve.)

EVIE. Oh, John, would you bring the scotch for our young friend here. He is in dire need of a drink. *(to DELL:)* How would you like it? *(DELL shrugs.)* Just the scotch. And then would you please go and chain the

dogs. Our other guest seems to have gone missing and ...
ah ... What is your name?

DELL. Me? Dell.

EVIE. Dell is of the opinion that Bill has been treed by
the Dobermans. He feels you are the one who should go
and take a look. *(JOHN, who has been standing behind DELL'S
back, grinning from ear to ear, bows and retires.)* Now then,
shall we talk? *(seeing the cracker in her hand)* Oh, I'm sorry.
Would you care for a cracker? *(DELL shakes his head.)* How
have you been passing the time up there?

DELL. Reading a bit. Comics mostly. Playing cards.
Watching out the window. I been playing with Dave quite
a bit. You know. Keeping him happy. Time goes.

EVIE. Dell ... that's an unusual name.

DELL. It's a nickname ... for Derek.

*(JOHN returns with a tray on which are a bottle of whiskey and
two glasses. He puts the tray down beside DELL.)*

DELL. Ta. *(JOHN goes. DELL, pouring himself a stiff whiskey.)* That guy really gives me the creeps. I don't know
which is worse, him or the bloody wolves out there.
Cheers. *(EVIE nods ackowledgement and DELL takes a swig.
He doesn't go into a coughing fit as HELENA did with the brandy,
but the whiskey does burn its way down his throat and he does a
miniature contortionist act.)*

EVIE. Better?

DELL. Ta. *(He takes another swig. This one is smoother.)*
Yeah ... that's great. *(He re-examines his sleeve.)* Will you
look at that? *(He lets out a whistle and then a laugh as a reaction
to his near escape. Then he looks at EVIE.)* You did get the

money didn't you? *(EVIE nods.)* I mean, what we saw you carry into the greenhouse was the money. Yeah, it had to be. We had a drink on that when we saw you.

EVIE. You even have drink up there?

DELL. Only beer. Cans of beer.

EVIE. A gourmet's paradise — baked beans and cans of beer. David won't be the only one farting fit to bust.

DELL. Hey? *(laughing)* You can say that again.

EVIE. Thank you, I don't wish to.

DELL. You know something? You're not a bad old stick at that. In fact, you're rather nice. You must be nice, to be able to say things like that, all natural like. I'm sorry about all this. You know. But ... well ... I mean, that's the way it goes, in'it? I mean, a guy's got to live.

EVIE. What are you going to do with your share of the money?

DELL. Live it up, lady. Live it up.

EVIE. I wouldn't have thought you had the taste for high living.

DELL. Well, as Bill says, I can always get one. *(He has poured himself another drink and now lifts his glass.)* Cheers. Oh, sorry. You want one?

EVIE. No thank you. Well, what shall we talk about now? *(DELL shrugs and takes another swig from his glass.)* I know. Why don't I show you my photograph albums? Would you like that?

DELL. Yeah. *(EVIE goes to her cupboard which she has to unlock to take out two or three albums.)* I like looking at photograph albums. People always want to apologize when they want to show them to you, but I like looking at them. I like to imagine things about people I see in pictures, faces an' that. I mean, you see a really good looking bird in a picture, you can ask all sorts of questions about her: Who's that? What's her name? How old is she? Where is she now? You know. And nobody really knows why you're asking.

EVIE. Well, I think you'll find these quite fascinating. Here, come and sit by me. We'll start with this one. *(DELL, accompanied by his glass, does as he is told and they settle down to look at the first album, EVIE holding it and turning the pages.)*

DELL. These are pretty old. They've gone all brown.

EVIE. These are of my childhood.

DELL. Which one's you?

EVIE. There.

DELL. You were very pretty. *(EVIE turns a page.)* Funny clothes.

EVIE. National costume.

DELL. What costume?

EVIE. German.

DELL. Oh, yeah. Those are what they call "leeder-hoosen," aren't they? Where's that?

EVIE. That is Berlin before the war. That is where we lived.

DELL. You mean you grew up in Germany?

EVIE. Yes. *(She turns the page.)*

DELL. Well you fooled me...

EVIE. I've fooled everybody.

DELL. I thought you were English, straight up.

EVIE. Everybody does.

DELL. You speak English very well.

EVIE. *(Turns the page.)* I made it my business to speak it perfectly. And imperfectly.

DELL. How d'ya mean?

EVIE. To speak it too perfectly might have been to give the game away.

DELL. What game? *(They have reached the end of the album. EVIE closes it and puts it down, picks up the second and passes it to DELL.)*

EVIE. The game of pretending to be something other than what I am. What I was. My husband knew of course, but what we had between us was something very special and that's another story. He saved my life. *(DELL has opened the album at the first page.)*

DELL. Who's that?

EVIE. My father.

DELL. Phaw! Look at that mustache. He's wearing one of those old spiked helmets.

EVIE. That was his dress uniform.

DELL. First World War was it?

EVIE. That's right. Iron Cross First Class and many other decorations.

DELL. A real hero. *(DELL turns the page. Silence. He turns another page. Silence. He turns another page. He looks up at EVIE who is sitting smiling at him. He looks down again, turns another page.)* What do you keep these for? In a photo album?

EVIE. They are photographs, aren't they?

DELL. I've seen some like this before. My grandad got some he brought back after the war. He used to keep them on top of his wardrobe so the kids couldn't see them.

EVIE. I have to admit, keeping some of these was rash,

but I couldn't help it. They reminded me ... *(DELL turns another page.)*

DELL. *(His voice is now hardly more than a whisper.)* Is that you?

EVIE. Yes.

(JOHN appears at the door to the house and stands there.)

DELL. What uniform is that?

EVIE. A commandant's uniform.

DELL. You mean ... you were in charge? Of ... of ... that place?

EVIE. That's right. *(For a long, awful moment, DELL stares at EVIE, trying to take in both what he has seen and heard.)*

DELL. Oh, my God ... I think I'm going to be sick. *(He gets to his feet and, as he turns to go, JOHN blocks his way. DELL stares at him for a second and then runs for it. JOHN grabs him, twisting one arm behind his back and holding him around the throat. DELL kicks and struggles but JOHN'S grip stays firm.)*

EVIE. Did you find Bill?

JOHN. *(Laughs.)* Of course I found Bill. We knew all along where he was, didn't we? *(to DELL:)* Do you want to see your Bill? Hmn? Shall we show him to you? *(He pushes the struggling DELL towards the cupboard. DELL is incapable of speech because of the pressure of the arm across his throat, but he struggles not to be taken to the cupboard where EVIE is now standing.)* Come on, boy. Don't you want to see your friend? Take a look.

(EVIE opens the cupboard doors. BILL is hanging from a coatpeg

by a butcher's hook thrust under his jaw. His hands are tied behind his back, there is a gag in his mouth. His torso is bare and both his face and body have been literally flayed by the pin-holder. His eyes stare out from a mass of unrecognizable, ribboned flesh. DELL stares at this horror and then makes a gigantic effort to free himself, which he does. He dashes for the door but JOHN catches up with him and grabs him again. They are close to the stove. EVIE shuts the cupboard. JOHN presses DELL'S face against the top of the stove. DELL screams. JOHN pulls him up. The side of the boy's face is one red and black burn. The skin left on the stove smokes blackly.)

JOHN. *(now absolutely vicious)* Not such a pretty boy now, hey? Not so pretty. *(He drags the almost gibbering DELL, a limp with fear lamb to the slaughter, around the corner of the conservatory. EVIE crosses to pick up and put away her photograph albums. Then she starts to butter herself another cracker. JOHN returns. He is splattered with blood.)* Like sticking a pig.

EVIE. Well ... so that is over.

JOHN. I'll put them in the attic. They can rot up there and no one will ever know.

EVIE. And, having got rid of them both, you can now enjoy the full fruits of your labor.

JOHN. Hey?

EVIE. Fifty thousand pounds is a lot of money, even in this day and age.

JOHN. What're you talking about? *(EVIE lifts the tray cloth and turns towards JOHN holding a .45 service revolver. JOHN stares at it in utter amazement.)*

EVIE. Do you think you fooled me for one moment? Why did you do it?

JOHN. Now look... wait... I don't know what you mean ... I swear I...

EVIE. You can stop playing the innocent. Today was supposed to be Peter's day off. He was never meant to pick up the money. You were. You didn't know he had asked me to change his day and, when he found the bag and was bringing it back here to me, questions would be asked. So you killed him and hid the bag. I ask you again — why did you do it? There was no need. Haven't I given you everything? Couldn't you wait for me to die?

JOHN. No. I couldn't. You old bitch. You'll go on forever. I'll never be free of you. What about a life of my own? Do you think I want to stay here? Tied to this place? To you? And how do I know, when you die, you'll leave everything to me? What about Penny? You said yourself I couldn't be sure. And what about that brat up there?

EVIE. Well, it has all been in vain. You didn't bother, I take it, to look inside the bag.

JOHN. What?

EVIE. Where would I have got fifty thousand pounds from?

JOHN. I saw you! In here! I saw you put the money in the bag!

EVIE. You saw me take some money, five hundred pounds to be exact, out of the bag and put it back. And I was hoping someone would see me do it. Do you think I can just walk into the small country branch of a bank and ask for fifty thousand over the counter? You are ridiculous. *(She raises the revolver in both hands.)*

JOHN. Mother! Don't!

(He turns to run and EVIE fires. JOHN hits the floor and lies there groaning. EVIE gets up, crosses to him, and calmly puts another bullet into him. She then walks into the house and starts up the stairs.)

EVIE. Helena ... Helena...

(The LIGHTS CHANGE and the CHILD NOISES are heard. EVIE disappears. The LIGHTS CHANGE back. There is the sound of HAMMERING on a far away door and, in the distance, ROLAND'S voice.)

ROLAND. Evie! Evie!

(Silence. Then ROLAND hurtles into the room from the garden door. He looks around, advances, sees JOHN. PENNY runs in. ROLAND has had a closer, if somewhat gingerly, look at JOHN. He looks up at PENNY who is staring in horror. PENNY turns away. ROLAND gets to his feet and looks around, completely at a loss as to what to do next.)

ROLAND. Can you hear anything? *(PENNY shakes her head. ROLAND calls.)* Evie! Evie!

(There is a TAPPING at the cupboard door.)

ROLAND. Did you hear that?

(The TAPPING is repeated. ROLAND goes to the cupboard and opens it. BILL is hanging on his hook. Slumped on the other side of the cupboard is DELL with his throat cut. In between them,

HELENA. She staggers/falls out of the cupboard. ROLAND jumps forward to catch her. PENNY is screaming. ROLAND puts HELENA down and quickly shuts the cupboard. Then he turns to PENNY and shakes her violently. PENNY'S screaming turns to sobbing. ROLAND holds her very tight for a second.)

HELENA. Evie ... upstairs ... Evie...

ROLAND. What?

HELENA. Evie ... David ... Evie ... upstairs...

ROLAND. *(turning back to PENNY)* For God's sake, Penny!

(Then he runs out and disappears into the house. There is the sound of GLASS being broken and he appears in the doorway with a double barrelled shotgun.)

ROLAND. Penny ... try ... try ... look after her ... stay here ... don't move from here. *(Then he turns and sprints up the stairs.)* Evie! *(PENNY crosses to HELENA and the two women huddle together for comfort.)* Evie!

(There is the sound of a SHOT. Silence. The sound of the CHILD NOISES can be heard and then the figure of EVIE is seen descending the stairs. She is carrying the shotgun. She stops at the entrance to the conservatory and looks at HELENA and PENNY. The shotgun is slowly raised. BLACKOUT. The gun is FIRED — both barrels.)

PROPS LIST

ACT I — 1
Furniture, as designed
Trug (Helena)
Basket of cut fall flowers (Helena)
Vases in cupboard, one to break each performance
Trick pruning knife for cutting John (Helena)
Handkerchief (Helena)
Rag in cupboard (Helena)
Watch or pin watch (Helena)
Tool belt for Bill, small
Telephone on upstage center wall, with enough cord so
    receiver can be taken into archway and conservatory
Morning paper, freshly folded (Helena)
Fresh large rose for Dell
Canvas tool holdall (Dell)
Small watering can (preset table SL)
Small handbell on table (preset)
Large Bandaid on John
Tray with coffee, milk, sugar, cups and saucers—
practical
    (Helena)
Watch (Roland)
Two more cups and saucers (Evie)

ACT I — 2
Holdall (Bill)
2 pinholder frogs (one fake) in cabinet
Handkerchief (Helena)
Decanter and 2 brandy glasses (Helena)

ACT II — 1
Book (Evie)
Key on a chatelaine (Evie)
Dressing in cupboard as indicated in script

ACT II — 2
Old carpet bag (Evie)
Wad of £5 notes in carpet bag
Broom out of closet (John)
Secateurs (John)
Coat and small suitcase (Helena)
Sewing basket out of cupboard (Evie)

ACT II — 3
Evie's book in cupboard (Helena gets)

ACT II — 4
Jacket over shoulder, Bill
Pc. of paper on telephone table (offstage center) (Evie)

ACT II — 5
Tray, covered with cloth, under which is a drumstick,
   other light food (Evie)
Tray with whiskey decanter, two glasses (John)
Two or three picture albums in cupboard (Evie)
.45 Service revolver on tray (Evie)

ACT II — 6
Double barreled shotgun (Roland)

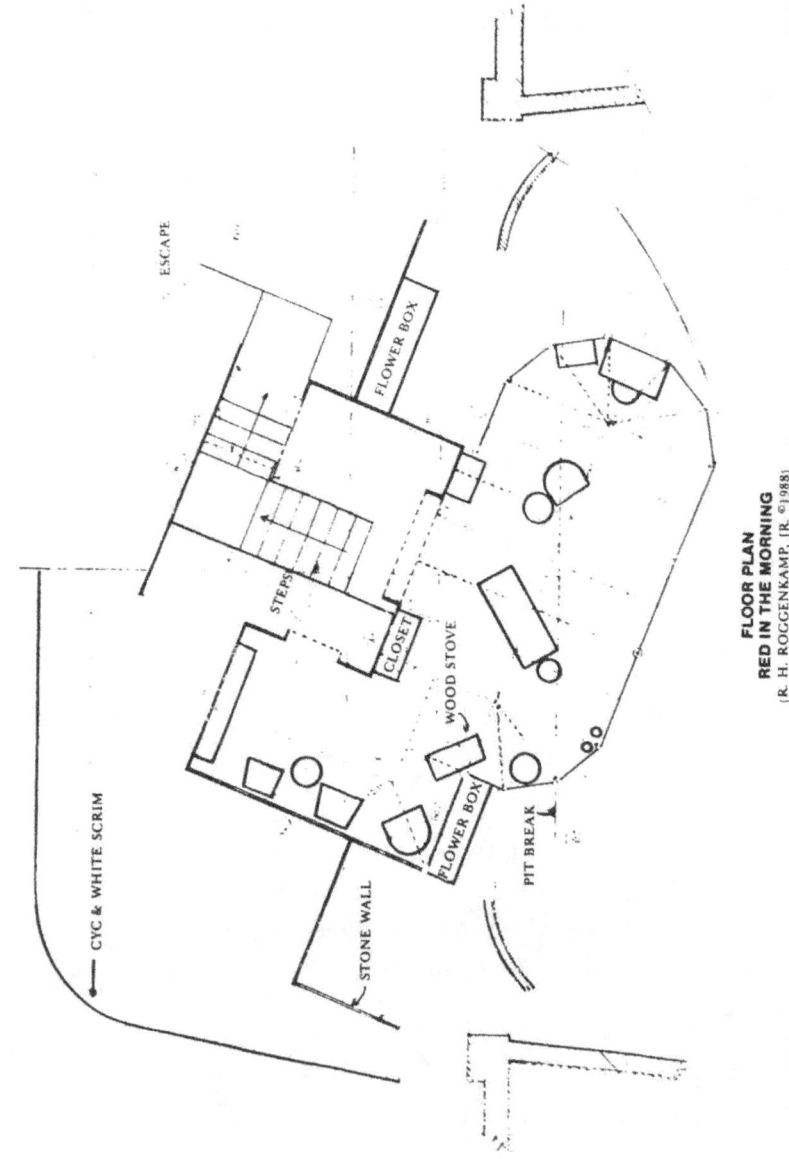

FLOOR PLAN
RED IN THE MORNING
(R. H. ROGGENKAMP, JR. ©1988)

ESCAPE

FLOWER BOX

STEPS

CLOSET

WOOD STOVE

FLOWER BOX

CYC & WHITE SCRIM

STONE WALL

PIT BREAK